MARATHON Wheeler

LIVING WITH PHYSICAL DISABILITY

MARA†HON Wheeler

LIVING WITH PHYSICAL DISABILITY

HEATHER S. COOMBES

Books to Life Marketing
KNOW YOUR BOOK'S PURPOSE TO LIFE

Contents

Dedicated to the memory of a faithful dad, Keith, to a loving mum, Shirley, a caring brother and sister-in-law, Malcolm and Carolyn, my fun-loving nephews and niece, Tim, Beth, Pete, and Chris, and to those brave souls, Amy, Lauren, and Andrew, who have joined our family through marriage.

Therefore, since we are surrounded by so great a cloud of witnesses, let us also lay aside every weight and the sin that clings so closely and let us run with perseverance the race that is set before us, looking to Jesus the pioneer and perfecter of our faith, who for the sake of the joy that was set before him endured the cross, disregarding its shame, and has taken his seat at the right hand of the throne of God.

—Hebrews 12:1–2 (NRSV)

Preface

Welcome to *Marathon Wheeler*. The experience of disability is not a "one size fits all" scenario. Each of us is unique, so this memoir, personal reflection, and collection of handy hints will not be helpful to everyone. Imagine you are in a department store with many items on display to tempt the buyer. Enjoy the experience of browsing. It is my hope that you will discover in these pages some insights you will find beneficial.

What would I like to achieve in writing this book?

1. The initial part of the book tells some of my story, from a Christian perspective as a person with cerebral palsy who spends a lot of time in a wheelchair. In sharing my experiences, I trust that you and others may see the possibilities of life and service in the midst of physical difficulty.

2. Chapter 14 concludes the narrative by tracing my understanding and experience of God, including an authentic view of life which deals with the toughness and blessings that meet me each day.

3. The appendices give practical ideas I have discovered along the way for people with physical disability. I hope they are of assistance as you reach your potential.

4.   The appendices also share practical hints for friends, carers, church members, and others who wish for a deeper understanding of the experience of physical disability.

It is my hope that in reading the words that follow, you find energy and breath to run, paddle, or wheel your marathon.

Heather Coombes
2016

Acknowledgements

Heartfelt thanks go to family and friends who encouraged me in this project, read the manuscript, and navigated me through the hissy fits of my computer.

Thank you to the staff of Westbow Press who have supported me through the production of this book.

Sincere efforts have been made to correctly attribute the sources of quotations and ideas wherever possible. Where I have failed to do so, I offer my apologies.

Warmest gratitude goes to Dr Robin Parsons for her faithful editing and restructuring of the manuscript. Final responsibility for the content remains with me.

Introduction

RETIREMENT AS AN aged care chaplain from UnitingCare Ageing Central Coast (New South Wales, Australia) offers me an opportunity to ponder on my experiences of life so far.

My first attempt at writing this book ended explosively when I lost thirty-three pages of a fledgling creation. My computer crashed, humming and flashing its contents into oblivion. The preciously crafted creation disappeared mysteriously into the ether. Fiery words hit the ceiling. It has taken me a year to begin again. There are echoes here of author Ernest Hemingway, who wrote a whole manuscript which he absent-mindedly left on a train, never to be seen again. Still, like all persevering writers, he picked himself up and began from the beginning—once more.

The importance of perseverance like this is a strong theme of the book. Its significance is reflected in the choice of title, *Marathon Wheeler*. Having a chronic disability requires that, like many others, I live with challenge for the long haul. The experience is not a quick sprint around the block. I, along with many, have to dig deep into God-given inner resources to live whatever years are granted to me with gutsy purpose.

This book is not written to boast that "I have made it" in the journey to live my life in a God-honouring way. I have a physical disability: cerebral palsy, in the moderate to severe range. Some have said to me,

"Isn't it great that you have accepted your disability and you have overcome your difficulties?" I prefer to see it as an ongoing pilgrimage. Even in my sixties, I get grumpy. I am still trying to make sense of physical challenge, occasionally rebelling against difficulties. I am in the process of overcoming, and I still struggle—hopefully with a touch of style. Until I breathe my last breath, my quest to live life faithfully with the circumstances that are mine will continue. So this is shared with you in the spirit of "one beggar telling another beggar where to find food."

While this book is written to encourage people with disability and their families, I hope that fellow travellers with different life experiences will find hope in it too. It is penned from a Christian perspective. I trust that this particular gentle lens, through which I look at the world, will be life-giving for other seekers also. Churches seeking to extend their ministry with mobility-challenged people may find it useful too. It is partly a memoir, partly a sharing of faith, and partly a practical toolkit for people with physical disability and their enablers on how to survive a different journey.

1

Rooted In Family

Family of Origin

WHILE TRAVELLING MY path of adventure, I do not move on alone. Mine is not a solitary existence. We, together, are made for community. In fact, there are many people who shape us. To borrow physicist Isaac Newton's expression, we stand on the shoulders of giants. Even famous, skilled people do not arrive at their destinations purely by pulling up on their own bootstraps. There are people who are our models—people who inspire and who influence us in big and small ways. Warren Buffett, a US financier, said, "Someone is sitting in the shade today because someone planted a tree long ago."[1]

I have reaped the benefits of the work and attitudes of people in my past and present. Let me share with you brief glimpses of the devoted people who influenced me to be the person I am today.

Grandparents

My positive relationships with grandparents were strong preparation for a later career in aged care. Each played his or her part in shaping my values and ministry. I learned from them as they faithfully lived their lives and faced challenges as age crept on. I also saw the effect of those difficulties on Mum and Dad as they cared for them.

Ma (Lily Coombes)—*Deaconess*

Ma's grey hair was always arranged in a tight bun. Crystal beads hung round her neck, one of the few concessions she made to wearing jewellery. A devout person, she lived simply and was born of strict Scottish Presbyterianism. Although my grandmother was not prone to excitement, her kindly brown eyes twinkled when something caught her fancy. Her clear sense of right and wrong emerged from a disciplined upbringing. Ma's ideal of sacrificial service was faithfully lived through her fingertips—a quality that shone as she stood by her man during missionary service in India. Ma's courtesy, generosity, and care toward her grandchildren seeped through her being.

Christianity was the root of her existence. In that spirit, she quoted, "As thy days so shall thy strength be" (Deut. 33:25 KJV). I recall the verse when I am tired. I am not given strength by God just for the years of my life, but for the days, the hours, and the minutes.

My grandmother taught me about grief. The tender respect she held for her beloved husband was strong, but it was only in her bereavement that I realized its depth. Imagine my surprise when we visited her as a new widow. Here was a strait-laced lady reading a romantic novel. Her pastime provided the reassurance of love she was sorely missing. Tears glistened in her eyes on another occasion as she waved goodbye to Mum and Dad, who were about to travel overseas. Perhaps she thought she might never see them again. These pictures of open grief softened my image of a strict grandma, making me sensitive to losses older people face as they surrender precious loved ones.

However, goodbyes are often followed by welcomes. My brother and sister-in-law brought their first newborn son to his great-grandmother. She held the little one (happily born on her husband's birthday) with a smile of delight on her wrinkled face. New life touched her tender heart.

Pa (Victor Coombes)—*Minister of Religion*

How does one paint a picture of this dedicated, dignified Christian who spent much of his life in church mission administration? Pa's skill in dealing with copious correspondence, coupled with conscientious stewardship of people's money, made him a diligent leader. His passionate advocacy in the public Christian arena and his understanding of Aboriginal people were qualities for which he is remembered. He was one of the members of the founding committee of NAIDOC Week (named for the National Aboriginal and Islander Day of Observance, now celebrated yearly in Australia). His precise mannerisms were tempered by bursts of humour. Pa had a deep appreciation of nature, including a love he shared with me of the fragrance of violets. During a visit to the family home, he sat by our record player, transfixed, listening to "I know that my Redeemer liveth" from Handel's *Messiah*. In an awed tone of voice, he exclaimed to me, "Isn't that grand?" Music nurtured his deep faith.

Nan (Eadith Brown)—*Tailoress*

Nan was a solid, good-humoured woman who rose above early challenges. In her teen years, she suffered typhoid fever. Her first fiancé was killed in the war. One can only imagine the effect such sorrow would have had, but she showed no hint of public grief. These experiences of illness and sadness speak of her inner strength.

Nan sang a song, "Knees Up, Mother Brown," exhorting me in a fun way to exercise my knees' flexibility on arm crutches. She was patient in teaching me to knit. My memories of Nan are frequently associated with food. Nan cooked luscious scones and home-made ice cream and orange jelly. Who could forget foraging for silver coins carefully hidden in her Christmas puddings? I proudly wear her gold wedding ring today—a sign for me of dedication to God and in loving memory of a woman whose heart was as big as the wide Australian outback.

Pop (Alfred Brown)—*Refrigeration Engineer*

Through the eyes of his grandchildren, sandy-haired Pop was normally a chirpy soul. His friendship with the younger generation was fun-loving.

Pop was skilled with his hands, which he used to create equipment for my disability. With designs from the Spastic Centre, he made a standing box and a stabilizer. These pieces of equipment enabled me to stand supported, knees straight, with the help of locked callipers or leg irons. The equipment encouraged correction of my usual S-shaped standing posture. When I was strapped upright into the stabilizer for a half hour each day, I played tennis with myself, hitting a ball against the wall.

The standing box enabled me to engage in activities while in a standing position. The metal callipers on my legs locked so that my naturally bent knees were forced straight, making it biomechanically easier to remain upright.

Pop also made wooden "skis," which were strapped to my ankles. They enlarged the surface area by which my feet touched the floor. I slid along like a cross-country skier without poles. It was good being able to walk unassisted this way for a short while.

Nan and Pop made a cheerful partnership. When Nan died, Pop was devastated. He did not want community or residential aged care. It was through Mum's practical support that his life was extended in years and quality. Mum's balance of caring responsibilities for her dad and her own family, though, involved careful negotiation. Such juggling was temporarily costly to her health. Her experience heightened my awareness of the difficulties middle-aged carers face in navigating conflicting expectations.

Pop enjoyed reminiscing. Hard financial times during the Depression were a recurring theme in his stories. Loss of jobs left him wondering where the next meal was coming from. He prayed earnestly to God. And a few days later, he would obtain employment—an answer to a heartfelt entreaty. These experiences led Pop to be frugal with money—a quality I have found invaluable for myself. I was heartbroken to say farewell to this genial storyteller.

Parents

Dad (Keith Coombes)—*Minister of Religion*

Born in India, Dad breathed the air of dedicated service that surrounded him. The Christian missionary culture espoused by his parents emphasized sacrifice of personal and family needs to the common good. Dad was sent to a boarding school in India at the age of five. He used to cry himself to sleep because he missed family life, craving the cuddles that parents give their children at bedtime. One wonders what scars of inferiority were seared on his heart because of this separation.

Years later after his marriage to Mum in Australia, Dad and she sailed back to India for a five-year stint of missionary service. After graduating from language school, Dad's role in the town of Sholinghur and environs included preaching, pastoring, and educational and mission administration.

How do you describe my father? Words like *humble, reliable, self-aware, gruff,* at times *tense, perfectionist, focused, driven,* and *punctual* come to mind. He made good use of time, hating to waste minutes. Occasionally, though, this dignified man lapsed into unexpected humour.

He was sometimes sensitive to thoughtless pinpricks. With a wry grin, he remarked occasionally, "You know that behind every silver lining there is a black cloud!" He balanced his pessimism well by encouraging his kids, who sometimes worried about the future. One of his sayings was, "It'll work out. Look in the past—God provided for you then, and he will provide for you now and into the future."

For all his emotional complexity, I loved him deeply. I believe that his deep pastoral sensitivity to those who struggled was born of his own wrestling to conquer the demons that taunted him on occasions.

Dad's nickname should have been Barnabas, an early Christian follower. The name means "son of encouragement." Barnabas boosted the new Christian convert Saul (later Paul), who was viewed with suspicion because Christians feared for their lives at his persecuting hands. Yet Barnabas saw Saul's potential and gave his support to Saul at a fragile time (see Acts 9:27). I appreciated my father's encouragement of those trying to improve their skills.

On one occasion, Dad was preaching at a remote church. The organist was a young farmer. His musical prowess left a lot to be desired as he hit more wrong notes than right. I was struggling to keep a straight face as I listened. To Dad's credit, he shook the organist's hand afterward, exclaiming, "Keep up the good work!" When I questioned him later, Dad said, "He's doing his best, and he deserves a go."

Academically minded, Dad was a thoughtful preacher. To ensure the relevance of his sermons, he was an avid reader of newspapers. His pastoral visiting combined a deep understanding of human nature and an intelligent wisdom about how to live life faithfully. Dad completed a thesis on Aboriginal reconciliation. Later in life, he graduated as a master of arts in spirituality. He also wrote unpublished Australian parables.

No one could doubt that he was a loving father. He used to pen a kiss and hug on my hand when I came into his study as a little kid. After mowing the lawn, sweat pouring off his brow, he handed me a tiny yellow flower in his big fingers. This tender gesture made me appreciate beauty in small things.

His affection for me was also expressed in other ways. Dad created comical stories to send me to sleep as a child. When I was in high school, he patiently coached me in algebra, using pieces of fruit to illustrate a point. After operations in my forties, I had torrid dreams about my body being wrenched open. Dad placed his hand on my forehead tenderly one evening. He prayed for me, saying afterwards, "You won't have nightmares tonight." He was right. Sleep enveloped me.

When I was away from home, Dad corresponded. He drew cartoon-like stick figures with humorous captions relating to my life at the time. Alternatively, he clipped out newspaper articles in which he thought I would be interested.

Dad was also a dedicated son to his ageing parents. He visited weekly, often accompanied by us. Visits to all grandparents strengthened our family ties. These connections laid vital foundations for my future pastoral ministry with ageing people.

How do I summarise the significance of Dad's life? His humble words say it all. At Dad's final district church meeting before retirement, all outgoing ministers were asked to say a few words. While those who spoke before him waxed eloquent, Dad's greeting was short and sweet: "God does not call us to be successful but to be faithful." You could have heard a pin drop. His words were few and full.

Dad's Death

Dad predicted he would not make old bones. When he died suddenly at home, I placed the sign of the cross gently on his forehead to send him on his way. His departure was a shock. Tears flowed. I was given a precious gift though. In a vivid dream, I saw Dad bending down, kissing me, sombrely yet tenderly saying "Ta-ta." I woke up shivering, yet deeply comforted. Was his spirit passing by me on his journey to the next life? He seemed so close.

What was life like after his funeral? Fragile, still processing our cataclysmic goodbye, I conducted a wedding of a mature couple and the funeral of an elderly resident within the next days. What a roller coaster of emotions this was! My function as marriage celebrant had to take supreme place over my own feelings. The couple were appreciative of my efforts to ensure a meaningful service.

My trip to the resident's funeral was complicated. With the Central Coast knee-deep in flood, I drove in the direction of the chapel through gushes of water. Would the car splutter into silence? Would I float away, never to be seen again? I rang the funeral director, saying that I might not make the service. He replied, "Keep trying. The celebrant from the service before yours can step in, if necessary."

A minister cannot let down a grieving family. I drove through torrents, peering through the storm-beaten windscreen, praying earnestly. My heart raced. My whitened knuckles gripped the steering wheel. With only two minutes to spare, I reached the chapel.

I conducted the funeral, aware that my heart, running on adrenaline, was vulnerable. My mourning, though, deepened my empathy for the relatives as they experienced their loved one's funeral.

Grief bit hard, leaving me wandering in a daze. Initially, it felt as if Dad had gone on a holiday and would return. This protective mechanism paved the way for the grim reality of physical absence. A year passed before I felt normal again.

Vivid dreams of a joyful Dad, however, reassured me in the midst of chaos. The last dream depicted him in a supermarket in the next aisle. He waved to us in a genial manner, but continued assisting shoppers. I interpreted his air of friendly detachment to mean that Dad's mission with us was complete. He had other tasks to fulfil.

A friend reminded me, "Look after that dear mum of yours!" Since then, Mum and I have kept a loving eye on each other. In the early days, though, it was difficult to know how much help was needed. New roles were negotiated. Mum assumed further responsibilities. Usually an energetic person, the new widow temporarily lost her umph. Mum needed space to feel her grief.

Little by little, a new normal evolved. We were further challenged when my brother and his family moved to Queensland. Our usual supports changed dramatically, but daily strength was granted to us on our rocky pathway.

I am thankful for Dad's loving legacy. The sting of absence has lessened. I admire his intellect, miss his sermons, and have high expectations of others' preaching. His death, however, helped me redefine a more autonomous faith, encouraging me to continue my reflection on the Christian life.

Mum (Shirley Coombes)—*Executive Secretary*

Mum was deeply committed to Dad, accompanying him to India as a young bride. I cannot overestimate Mum's courageous sense of adventure as she accommodated to a different culture. High population density, heat, noise, basic living challenges, work with servants, monkeys on trains, and a different language were all part of her new reality. Getting used to novel food and customs; being exposed to

Hinduism, with its colourful religious festivals; and being encouraged to ponder the issues of caste and the extremes of poverty and wealth were part of her everyday experience.

My mother rode an elephant through the Mysore State Forest while on holiday. She remembers riding a bicycle down hills through crowded towns, trying to dodge people, cows, and other animals. Mum and Dad sometimes rode in horse-drawn vehicles, *jutkas*, similar to those driven by the Amish. As a newly married missionary in Sholingur, Mum became temporary house-mother to a girls' boarding school.

I asked her once whether she was frightened during these different experiences. She replied, "No, not with Dad at my side. He was my rock."

On their return to Australia, Mum worked voluntarily in churches as receptionist, organist, women's group president, fete organiser, hostess, caterer, and devotional speaker. The Spastic Centre (now Cerebral Palsy Alliance) also gained from her support.

Mum is optimistic, chatty, loyal, and reliable. Her eye is quick to spot need, and neighbours appreciate her support. Her common sense and problem-solving abilities are qualities I admire. Mum is my cherished friend, devoted to her family, and hospitable in nature.

She does not give up in the face of difficulty. Two of her common slogans are "Just do it" and "Do it now." Underneath her tender understanding, there is a steely determination which has stood her in good stead. Her easy chuckle was a foil to Dad's seriousness. Mum's energy is legendary. She does not know how to walk, only run.

She has been my voluntary physiotherapist, helping with prescribed exercises, supervising walking, and stretching tight muscles. Her love was tough. If I fell, hurting my leg, she urged me to get up. I did not appreciate this seeming lack of sympathy, but it helped me to grow resilience.

In her eighties, Mum learned to email and Skype to keep in touch with family. Flexible to change, she says that she will not let anything beat her. A motto oft heard from her lips is "If you don't use it, you lose it." She is not one to easily ask for help, wanting to master the skills necessary for the job at hand.

After her marriage, Mum did not return to the paid workforce. Family, church, and community owe her a debt of gratitude for countless hours of voluntary service. Dad paid her a family tribute by having a golden medal made in honour of her faithful servant heart.

Brother (Malcolm Coombes)—*Minister of Religion*

My brother is a kind and generous soul. He is responsive to those in need. Reserved in nature, he keeps his cards close to his chest. He views life through a logical lens, tempered with compassion. He is a man of few words, but his thoughtful actions speak thunderously loud. He ploughs himself into his vocation with determined focus.

One of my teenage recollections of my brother is associated with the dissection of a rat. As a correspondence student, I did not have access to dead animals while I was learning anatomy. A science teacher obtained a deceased rodent for me from her school. I started the dissection process carefully in the backyard. I was fascinated by the creature's intestines. I pulled them out to look more carefully. My brother sneaked up, scooped the entrails up, and placed them down his squirming sister's back. Butter wouldn't melt in his mouth! My loud screeches were heard throughout the neighbourhood.

During youth parties, Mal swung me round the dance floor. Our twirling might not have been the most graceful, with my tight-mus-cled legs refusing to coordinate. In fact, I must have looked like a sack of potatoes from Flemington Markets. However, I was in my seventh heaven, experiencing a touch of teenage normality. I thought my beloved brother was the best thing since strawberry ice cream!

In later years, it was an honour for me to be one of the bridesmaids at Mal and Carolyn's wedding. The night before the big event, accompanied by friends, I walked along a footpath on my Canadian crutches. Without warning, I fell down the gutter, resulting in a black eye. This was not the best scenario for a bridesmaid wanting to be a ravishing beauty for the nuptials.

While bride and bridesmaids were dressing the next day, a powder puff was dabbed around my eye to cover a multitude of sins. Later, I was the first bridesmaid, inching my way nervously down the aisle while clutching my brightly coloured bouquet on the handle of one of my Canadian crutches. Joy of joys, I managed to stay upright this time! It was a happy day for the bridal couple and guests.

After the exciting adrenaline rush, reality set in. I realised how much life would change because family was now scattering.

In a pensive state of mind, I returned to Canberra. Taking a taxi from the airport, I asked my driver to carry a suitcase to my room. He returned with a decidedly quizzical look on his face. It was only when I trotted down to my domicile that I realised the reason. Friends had decorated my room with beer cans, streamers, and a sign on the door proclaiming, "My eyes are dim, I cannot see. I've been in the pub since half past three!" I laughed at this teasing reference to my topsy-turvy encounter with the gutter before the wedding. Any sombre homesickness I felt was dismissed.

Years have passed since those memorable departures and new beginnings. Now in mature adulthood, Mal can speak in public profoundly, his skills refined through his pastoral and educational profession. Teaching and preaching are his undeniable gifts—a chip off the old block, but with his own unique style.

His teasing keeps me humble. Returning from the hairdresser's one day, I modelled a new, cropped hairstyle. He laughed and for the next week called me "Shaving Brush." His brotherly humour has helped balance me when life gets too serious.

He also challenges me psychologically when I am frustrated with limitations. When a fear of falling gripped me as I was reaching for a face washer, I asked him to get it. He said, "I would travel miles if you needed help, but I reckon you can get the washer yourself." I retrieved the item after effort, but thanks to him, I had been discouraged from a life of learned helplessness.

Mal urged me strongly one day, "Don't apologise for your struggle." I had just uttered several agonised "Sorrys!" in the belief that my slow movement had been delaying people. It has been said, "Some days are diamonds. Some days are stones." That day, there were a profusion of not just stones, but jagged rocks thundering around my head, crushing any fragile positive thoughts struggling to find expression. Sometimes, there is no energy for the heroine to emerge.

I wonder about the impact on siblings whose family is touched with disability. Their sensitivities and perhaps even their sacrifices need to be honoured. How did reflective Mal cope when attention was diverted to my medical needs? A quiet achiever, he does not grab the limelight. What I have observed is how willing he is to be helpful in his wide circle of influence. Bravo to my wonderful brother, a true companion in arms!

Sister-in-Law (Carolyn Coombes)—
Occupational Therapist

Nine-year-old Carolyn, with a cheeky grin, first visited our home as one of the church families at Northbridge. After a platonic friendship, cemented in youth group years later, Mal and Carolyn eventually became romantically involved. Though sharing my brother was an adjustment for me, I was happy when they announced their engagement. I took a keen interest as they proudly waved Carolyn's diamond engagement ring in the air. The relationship is an attraction of opposites, Mal being a quiet introvert and Carolyn a blazing extrovert. However, they share a Christian faith, a genuine care for people, and a deep commitment to family.

Carolyn allowed this devoted aunt to cuddle, chat with, and read to their little ones. Whenever I have stayed with them, she has ensured that their house is accessible. Using her occupational therapy skills, she has also advised me on wheelchair and equipment design.

Endowed with a keen sense of justice and a desire to help those whose lives are difficult, Carolyn assisted members of the deaf community. She learned Auslan hand-signing language and often interpreted worship services in their local church. Later, Carolyn was passionately involved in refugee advocacy. Putting their money where their mouths are, Mal and Carolyn hosted two asylum-seeking boat people in their home for months. The experience was a learning curve for the whole family. They developed sensitivity to political issues and experienced the human face of what it is like to escape persecution. Carolyn also used her artistic bent to strengthen community links, organising craft groups.

Carolyn's strong organisational skills, dynamic energy, and hospitable heart are helpful qualities. Their house is often full of people: old friends, new friends, and strangers alike. In the midst of community involvement, Mal and Carolyn raised four fun-loving kids, who have compassion for those who have a tough start in life. I am proud that they have grown into capable leaders—a tribute to the investment their parents have made in their upbringing.

Left to Right:

First (front) Row: Heather, Chris (nephew)
Second Row: Peter (nephew)

Third Row: Mum, Beth (niece), Carolyn, Mal
Fourth Row: Dad, Tim (nephew)
Photographer: David Robertson

2

Fragile Beginnings

Birth

ON A FRIDAY evening at 5:45 p.m. in August 1954, I was born in a mighty hurry in the mission-based Scudder Memorial Hospital in Ranipet, South India. The fact that I was born two months premature was a cause for concern. My birth weight was only three pounds (1.36 kg). After birth, I was given two smallpox injections to vaccinate against this dreaded disease. I became very ill, to the point I almost died. But I have been told that girl babies are traditionally more able to survive birth difficulties.

The exact causes of my later-diagnosed cerebral palsy are still a mystery.

End of the Indian Chapter

While they continued to work in India, Mum and Dad took sought medical opinions on my condition. Doctors were not able to offer much help, other than to prescribe supportive shoes. They advised that it was not wise for me to stay in India long-term, because high humidity would make my mobility strained and energy sapping. Armed with that knowledge, Mum and Dad returned to Australia with their two-year-old. Here they waited for the impending birth of their second child.

A specialist finally diagnosed me with cerebral palsy. The doctor reassured Mum that there was no need to worry about the health of her forthcoming little one. She eventually gave birth to a healthy, red-haired boy, Malcolm Keith—a cause for great celebration.

Definition of Cerebral Palsy

I digress briefly from my story to offer an explanation of my medical condition. According to the Cerebral Palsy Alliance:

> Cerebral palsy (CP) is a physical disability that affects movement and posture. It is a permanent life-long condition, but generally does not worsen over time. It is due to damage to the developing brain either during pregnancy or shortly after birth.
>
> Cerebral palsy affects people in different ways and can affect body movement, muscle control, muscle coordination, muscle tone, reflex, posture and balance.
>
> People who have cerebral palsy may also have visual, learning, hearing, speech, epilepsy and intellectual impairments.
>
> What causes cerebral palsy?

Cerebral palsy is the result of a combination of events either before, during or after birth that can lead to an injury in a baby's developing brain.

There is no single cause of cerebral palsy. For most babies born with cerebral palsy, the cause remains unknown. Researchers now know that only a very small percentage of cases of cerebral palsy are due to complications at birth (e.g. asphyxia or lack of oxygen). Today, it is accepted that cerebral palsy usually arises from a series of *causal pathways*, i.e. a sequence of events that when combined can cause or accelerate injury to the developing brain.

For example: Although prematurity is the largest risk factor for cerebral palsy, it is the sequence of events (causal pathways) that led to the premature birth that may have caused the cerebral palsy, rather than the premature birth itself. In 13 out of 14 cases of cerebral palsy in Australia, the brain injury leading to cerebral palsy occurs either in the uterus (while the mother is pregnant) or before 1 month of age.

At present, the cause is not well understood for most of these babies. Stroke is the most common cause in babies who acquire cerebral palsy after 1 month of age. The stroke may occur spontaneously or arise from surgical or heart complications.

For further information, please see the Australian Cerebral Palsy Alliance website: *www.cerebralpalsy.org.au*

How Cerebral Palsy Affects Me Personally

Each person experiences cerebral palsy differently. My speech is slightly slower and perhaps more deliberate than that of most able-bodied people. Handwriting and computing are part of my skill set, but the pace again is slower. I am very sensitive to loud or sudden noises, having an exaggerated startle response. For this reason, as a child I disliked chiming grandfather clocks and bursting balloons. Firework displays with accompanying explosions fill me with horror because my whole body jolts in protest.

My muscles have always been tight, and I find it difficult to move freely or fast. Walking for me is strained partly because of bent knees.

Physios tell me that bent knees do not provide the best biomechanics for energy-efficient movement. As a young child, my leg muscles were underdeveloped. My lower limbs were and are weak, moving as if I am carrying a lead weight. In my early years, I used full arm crutches and wore full leg-length, ugly metal callipers. Lack of sustained energy resulted in my inability to walk great distances. I ran out of puff easily. Throughout my life, my upper body, shoulders, and arms have fortunately been strong enough to compensate, even with the presence of a pronounced curvature of the spine.

As my physical needs have changed, so has my equipment. At age twelve, I received my first manual wheelchair as a supplement to my walking—a wonderful gateway to freedom. I was able to travel farther to recreation, education, and holiday venues, opening up the world to me. In younger to middle life, my walking mobility progressed from full arm crutches to Canadian crutches, which gave me forearm support while walking. As I began aged care chaplaincy in my forties, I moved to a motorised wheelchair, which conserved my energy for pastoral tasks. In later life, when arthritis has affected my left knee and two shoulders, I primarily use a motorised chair for indoor mobility, a manual chair transported on top of my car when

I am out and about, and a forearm-support walking frame for home exercise only.

Fatigue is a common companion because of the effort involved in moving and because of medication side effects. I complete strenuous tasks when my energy level is higher. When tiredness sets in, I rest for a few minutes. When action is necessary, even in exhaustion, my strong will is a blessing.

3

Security and Strangeness

Young Years

FOLLOWING THE BIRTH of my brother, Dad became minister to the Presbyterian Church in Young, a rural town in New South Wales. A kaleidoscope of memories tumble in my mind as I reflect on childhood days, including open fires in winter, chilblains, and learning to knit. My fascination with the beauty of the natural world flourished while playing in the backyard. There are photographs on the lens of my mind's eye of a robin redbreast sitting on a fence. I made daisy chains in spring under the sprawling pepper tree, and patted the neighbour's gentle brown cocker spaniel. I was transfixed by the minuteness of orange-and-black-speckled ladybirds crawling on flowers. We cultivated crimson, pink, purple, mauve, and white sweet peas. Their breathtakingly sweet fragrance was enticing to my young nostrils. Because raising chooks was another family hobby, collecting eggs for our breakfast was a daily family routine.

Simple rituals bring great pleasure and provide glue for family stability. We drove in the country, stopping by the side of the road under the shade of tall gum trees. The rattle of cellophane paper heralded the opening of the lolly packet, and Minties would then be distributed. Home-cooked lemon meringue pies were devoured during other family festivities at a nearby dam. A sense of adventurous independence surrounded me as I walked on arm crutches with Mal to the corner shop to buy musk sticks and groceries. Because my physical activity was limited, I learned to enjoy simple pleasures.

Family games were played in the evenings, hide and seek being a favourite. Dad also played his "magic key" trick by the cosy flames of an open fire. He placed a big silver key in a white hanky, folded it carefully, and intoned, "Abracadabra." We closed our eyes to absorb the mystery. After time elapsed, he unfolded the hanky to discover the key was missing. Our task was to locate it, only to find it hidden behind a nearby chair. Our wide-eyed innocence did not plumb the depths of swift-handed illusion.

After minor family spats, the kids threatened to run away from home! One can imagine me hobbling down the main street on arm crutches with a swag on my back. Mum flattened me by asking Her High and Mightiness, "Do you want help packing your bag?" The prospect of going without her cooking made my brother and I rethink our strategy.

The family kitchen attracted many visitors, including the young milkman and the friendly grocer, each making home deliveries. Dad's farming parishioners also delivered produce. A minister's wage was not high, but people's generosity made up for scarcity of money.

One morning, Mum sniffled and wiped back her tears as she put on my leg callipers. I asked "What's wrong?"

She only said, "I am tired."

Was this unsettling grief around the daily challenge of caring for a child with a disability? A young, rural mum, a long way from her family of origin, bringing up two kids—one with special needs—would sometimes find life tough. I take my hat off to her sheer gutsiness.

Such courage would be further tested when I was admitted to hospital at five years old for an operation on my ankles. My walking had been characterised by moving on tippy toes. My Achilles tendons were contracted and needed to be released by surgery to enable better flat-footed walking. Happily, the operation was successful, but not without its emotional cost.

Hospital and Convalescence

We travelled seven hours to the children's hospital, an old building with brown, musty-toned walls. Mum and Dad stayed near until after the operation. After their farewells, my heartfelt crying pierced their hearts. No loving parents want to abandon their child. When they returned to Young, my dedicated grandparents assumed visiting duties. The memory of Nan bringing me a bright orange nasturtium holding a tiny snail is as clear as a bell. When I was moved to a rehabilitation centre, Pa visited, taking me out in the sunshine. Under the shade of giant trees, he fashioned a sword and sheath out of pine needles to help me do battle with the world. I was fascinated.

Travel distance, Dad's work commitments, and Mum keeping the home fires burning meant they could only visit periodically. On one occasion, I straightened my knees while lying in bed and curled down my toes in an excited muscular spasm (often typical of cerebral palsy) when I suddenly saw my dad's big smile and black curly head pop round the corner of the ward.

Sadness enveloped my heart at this time. I collected date numbers, which I painstakingly cut out from calendars with plastic scissors. I placed my treasures with great care into a tin. One day, my treasure chest clattered to the floor, beyond my reach. The cleaner picked it up and opened it. Puzzled at the contents, she whisked it away. I never saw my precious cargo again.

My eyes stung. I tried to be brave, without success. My hard work had disappeared like vapour. In my five-year-old nervousness, I could not explain how precious it was to me. A lump still rises in my throat as I write this.

Bathing in a warm bath after my plasters were removed is another terrifying memory. With waves of deep water splashing around me, I felt as if I were drowning. This was a fitting metaphor for my little life of helplessness.

I was comforted a little by cuddling my dolls. Yet separation from family casts a long shadow. A photo taken at the time of me with a glum expression captures it all. Nevertheless, my loving grandparents' occasional presence reassured me in a lonely time.

Infants' School

My return home ushered in a new era—going to school for the first time. The nurturing teacher calmed my first-day nerves, assuring us, her "little people," that there were no tigers to be scared of.

I am grateful for the education experiences I had as a child with disability in a rural mainstream school. No big deal was made of my impairments as I waddled along with full-length arm crutches. It was just expected that I was part of the class, with supportive friends. I was allocated two classmates each week to fetch anything I might need.

One day I had a holiday from my callipers, and my schoolmate didn't even notice. The heavy metal supports obviously did not loom large in her mind. Another friend eagerly reported to Mum one afternoon, as Mum came to collect me from school, "Mrs Coombes, Heather ran (on her crutches) today."

There are memories of warm pot-bellied stoves and icy fingers and toes at school in winter. In first class, we repetitively learned our vowels and spelling from an intense, newly graduated teacher. One of her favourite entreaties, regarding pupils who didn't always grasp what she was on about, was "Give me strength!" The words sounded like a frustrated prayer to her Almighty.

Photographer: Shirley Coombes

As seen through the eyes of a little child, Young engendered a life-long appreciation of rural life, a welcoming sense of community, and admiration for beautiful country scenery. Famity was strong, disciplined, safe, and loving.

4

Growing Up Fast

West Wollongong Years

I SHOWED AN early interest in creative writing as we moved homes. I enjoyed crafting compositions at mainstream West Wollongong Primary School. To call them literary works is a vast exaggeration. My conclusions to these fanciful stories were barely imaginative. Any family adventures I recorded were drawn together at the end by the words, "After a happy day, the family arrived home and had tea."

This lifelong love affair with stories and reading was fuelled by Mum and Dad reading bedtime stories to my brother and me. The fanciful characters in *Winnie-the-Pooh*, Enid Blyton's Noddy books, "Cinderella," and *The Enchanted Wood* appealed to my childish imagination.

My favourite Bible story at that point was about an ostracized tax collector, Zacchaeus, climbing a tree to see Jesus. (See Luke 19:1–10.) Why did the story resonate so much? Perhaps it was because Zacchaeus was an outsider—a man who was different yet welcomed warmly by Jesus.

Mal and I sometimes presented puppet shows for our long-suffering parents and grandparents. A faint scar on my brother's thumb reminds us of how we tried to make a stage out of a cardboard box. The pocket knife we used to carve holes in the box for the puppet strings slipped, resulting in blood flow from my sibling. On another occasion, at my grandparents' home, we staged a Christmas show. I knitted a red garter-stitch Santa's hat for one of our characters. Were we frustrated actors? No, we just wanted to have fun.

During piano lessons, I ploughed through musical scales and childish tunes, slowly deepening my appreciation of the creative arts. Sadly, after later operations, I could not get close enough to the piano to play it, because of my fused hip. However, my basic music knowledge helped me plan worship as chaplain in aged care facilities.

This pleasant childhood life was again disrupted when my left hip dislocated, making it difficult for me to walk without a severe limp and wincing pain. Following instructions from the Spastic Centre, every night Mum bandaged my legs to a metallic frame placed on my bed. The contraption was designed to spread my legs out and relocate my left hip in a better position. After this procedure, I could not move my legs or turn over; I had to remain flat on my back. Hours later, I would wake up in tears, leg muscles spasming, and my hip would scream out its presence. Mum had to undo bandages, remove the cumbersome metal contraption, and put me back to bed normally to relieve the pain. Her steadfastness was amazing. When I reflect on my mum and dad's devotion, it makes me realise that love is not a mere emotional feeling, but a series of decisive, committed actions for the welfare of family.

Hospital in Sydney

Orthopaedic surgery for people with cerebral palsy was common practice in 1965 and 1966, when I was eleven and twelve respectively. Before planned operations on my knees and, later, my hip, I asked my folks, "After this, will I be able to walk (unaided)?"

Their answer was, "We'll see." I appreciate now their willingness to be open-ended about the future.

I spent two separate long periods in a large hospital. The first experience involved bilateral knee operations, which necessitated plaster from thighs to ankles on both legs, in 1965. This was in an effort to straighten my bent knees to make my walking more effortless.

In 1966, the second long hospital stay involved having a left hip arthrodesis (a pin inserted into the hip to secure the ball into the damaged socket). The operation resulted in my being bedridden, lying on my back or stomach. I was in plaster for five months from the waist down to my left ankle.

Fortunately, after the hip operation, I had no pain. You could not wipe the grin from my face. However, I could not bend easily in the middle, and my existing curvature of the spine was exacerbated over time due to my changes in posture.

Combined efforts from a hospital schoolteacher, who supervised my lessons, and my regular teacher at West Wollongong, who sent packages of work by mail, enabled me to continue my education. I learned to write using an angled bed tray, as I lay on my back. Pencils were easier to use. Why? Ink at the writing end would dry up as the supply in the barrel moved to the other end of the pen, which I had to hold at a downward angle.

Compassionate health professionals are worth their weight in gold. Many an anxious moment in the children's ward was spent being mesmerised by glassy-eyed goldfish with pursed lips swimming round in a big tank in the ward. Using this familiar image, one good-humoured nurse coached me to drink a cup of water from a lying-down position without spilling it. She had the temerity to nickname me "Fish-Face." Laughter at my new identity caused me to splutter gushes of water down my front.

Another Christian nurse carefully wrote in my autograph book, the apostle Paul's words to the Philippians: "I can do all this through him [Christ] who gives me strength" (Phil. 4:13 NIV). This verse provided me with inspiration to keep going then, as it does now. Nurses like these were gems who lightened tough moments.

In those days, children were not allowed to visit hospital wards. For four weeks, I couldn't see Mal. I missed him and had to be content with seeing him once from the hospital window, waving to me uncertainly as he stood with Dad on the grass a few storeys below. However, Mum and Dad visited faithfully. The click of Mum's opening handbag was a comforting, domestic sound as I anticipated receiving small treats. The fragrance of one such gift—a small bottle of eau de cologne—arouses pleasurable memories.

Mostly, Mum appeared cheerful, in what must have been trying circumstances. However, my mother was in tears once, after a regimental sister-in-charge, dressed in a grey uniform and starched veil, reprimanded her for a minor infringement of strict hospital rules. Thank goodness, hospitals are now more family friendly. Was it any wonder that I was bursting out of my skin to leave hospital after what seemed to be an interminable time?

MacLeod House

I arrived by ambulance at MacLeod House, Allambie Heights, a residential facility for young people with cerebral palsy. The purpose of my transition to this facility was to undergo rehabilitation and continue my education. My first impressions of the building were very positive. The outside gardens housed colourful flowers amid manicured lawns. The girls' dorm was light and airy, housing twelve small beds with pretty floral bedspreads.

Despite the initial glow surrounding this non-hospital-like setting, I was not prepared for the psychological onslaught when my new roommates arrived back from school. Not to put too fine a point on it, I was dead scared of the residents. It was not their fault, of course. I simply had no previous experience of people with cerebral palsy in a more severe form than my own. Confronted with speech impediments and involuntary dribbling due to tongues hanging out, I simply could not understand them. Some of them had athetosis (involuntary muscular spasms of arms and legs). In those first days, my frightened mind thought they were from another planet. It was not uncommon for anyone, including me, who got too close to get unintentionally punched in the face. These involuntary movements were often exacerbated if the residents were nervous or under stress.

In what follows, I will use fictitious names for my roommates, to protect their privacy, Big, welcoming Pat had blonde, frizzy hair, a large mouth, and even larger teeth. I thought she was going to eat me for supper. She was one of the first to inch over to my bed. She used her unsteady hands to propel her manual wheelchair slowly towards me. I was too traumatised at the time to see her hospitable heart as she tried to welcome me. I could not understand her breathy, hesitant speech.

I edged—in heavy plaster, mind you—to the other side of my already narrow bed to try and get away from her. Luckily, I did not fall out, thanks to strategically placed bedrails.

On that first night, I earnestly prayed to God. "Get me out of here, quick. But if not … let me figure this out … I only have eighty-three more nights before I go home."

I ended up in residence for about six months. Because I had no choice, I stayed put. Little by little, day after day, I began to interpret the speech patterns, ignore the involuntary punches and the dribbles. Underneath the idiosyncrasies, their unique personalities emerged.

Here were kids who swore, who laughed, who were vulnerable, who missed their families, who were stubborn.

Aliens turned slowly into my dear friends with names: Pat, Cheryl, Jonesy, Joanne, Marie, and the rest. What a huge learning curve. I had to grow up quickly. As time crept by, some nurses thought I was fourteen. In fact, I was only eleven.

At 4:30 p.m., we ate our evening meal in the communal dining room. After graduating from being bedridden to sitting in a chair, I assisted my dorm mates with feeding, if they could not do it themselves. In the event they wanted to dictate letters home, I acted as scribe. Giving was not one way though. One of the girls was from New Caledonia. She helped me learn French, sometimes correcting my Aussie accent. Precious two-way friendships matured over time.

There were some funny episodes too. Diane, a friendly woman with cerebral palsy, walked stiffly up to me on her crutches and recounted a conversation her mother and her neighbour enjoyed. To put the conversation into context, it is helpful to know that one of the synonyms for cerebral palsy historically has been *spastic*. Spastic has gone out of favour because some used it as a derogatory term. Diane recalled the neighbour asking her mum, "How is your plastic daughter?" We both roared with laughter, trying to imagine what we would look like if made out of transparent material.

Bedridden and still encased in plaster from the waist down, I remember gazing out of windows while waiting for teachers, nurses, and physios. I imagined pictures in the clouds as they wafted across the bright blue sky. Having a disability requires patience. At the mercy of others' timetables, I discovered that the art of contemplating the ordinary was a handy skill.

Staff Tribute

Although waiting for staff loomed large in my life, I pay tribute to the dedicated women who worked with us. Sister Tulloch was a conscientious registered nurse, faithfully attending to the physical needs of her charges. A resident and I wrapped up a crumbly chocolate crackle in a white tissue to give her a holiday present. Normally a serious person, Tull giggled when presented with our gift. I still exchange Christmas cards with her and was delighted to see a recent photo of her with a ninetieth birthday cake. Sister Hamilton was a big, cheery registered nurse. We loved her to bits. She reminds me now of the archetypal Earth Mother.

Irene was a young woman with a cheeky grin and mischievous glint in her eyes. During the latter part of my recovery, she was assigned the task of dressing me in a blue-and-white spotted dress. The occasion was a party, the first one I had attended in many months. Cinderella's chariot was not a pumpkin. My "carriage" was a special chair with a horizontal support to hold up my left leg in a splint. Irene showed me how to put lipstick on for the first time. I applied copious amounts of fragrant hairspray to my carefully brushed hair and checked the final touches in my hand-mirror. All were necessary stages to mark an exciting rite of passage. I felt suddenly all grown up.

Sister Smith was our gentle Maori matron for a period. When she arrived at our dorm one night, we asked her to sing the Maori song of farewell, "Now is the hour when we must say goodbye." She sat on the bed and sang exquisitely. Her soulful, liquid brown eyes were framed by straight, black, shiny hair. I would not have been surprised if she was homesick. Did I imagine the moonlight illuminated her face as she serenaded us?

Flutterings of Fun

From fond memories of staff, I move now to special events. One lasting recollection I have is bumping up and down in a rattling Spastic Centre bus to attend the Moscow State Circus. I gazed with awed breathlessness at the bright lights under a huge tent, the sparkling pink costumes, the death-defying acrobatics, and the agile high-wire acts. Such a glittering spectacle provided a rare, welcome respite from the humdrum existence of physio, school, and institutional living. Viewing these feats of human flexibility might have exacerbated any loss I felt in comparing the artists' moving bodies to my locked joints and muscles. On the contrary, I was able to enjoy vicariously the experience of free movement. Even today, I exult when I see performances of graceful ice dancing, ballet, swimming, or gymnastics. The human body, when it glides well, is a joy to behold.

What other events gave me pleasure? I looked forward to Saturday family visits. Otherwise, weekends were painfully boring. Faithful schoolmates from my mainstream primary school sent cards and gifts through the mail. Apparently, the local newsagent did a roaring business in greeting cards. This enormous splurge of generosity did a mighty job to lift my spirits and kept me connected with the outside world. An elder of Dad's congregation and his wife visited the hostel and sent comics and fun magazines regularly. The reading added life to dull out-of-school hours. I could not believe such kindness and was not surprised when Dad called the thoughtful couple "the salt of the earth." Their practical ministry hit the spot.

Faith Forming, Learning, and Exercising

Sincere, local Baptist Sunday school teachers visited on Sundays to give lessons on Christianity. On one occasion they asked me a very pointed question. "Are you a Christian?" I felt like a cornered animal. "Half and half" was my considered yet evasive response.

In those days, God was my close companion in prayer, but I equated being a good Christian with experiencing only positive feelings—hence my non-committal answer to a forthright question.

My secular education progressed during the week, beginning each day with being wheeled in my bed down to a medium-sized classroom on-site. Nine children of varying disabilities worked at their own pace on different subjects. The atmosphere was friendly and light-hearted, largely due to the efforts of the teacher and teacher's aide.

In 1965, a smiling grey-haired woman of sixtyish years became my teacher during my first sojourn at the hostel. Her sense of humour added sparkle to the day. She made up hilarious stories to help me practice my spelling and dictation skills. Occasionally she wondered what would happen next in her meandering flights of fantasy, exclaiming to me, hands up in the air, "I've lost the thread of my dishcloth." Soon after she would gather her creative thoughts and resume the weaving of her wonderful stories.

The next year, during my second rehabilitation period at the hostel, we had a fun-loving, twenty-five-year-old teacher. She had jet-black curly hair and twinkling eyes. Her bouncy personality lit up the schoolroom.

Agonising physiotherapy was a necessary part of my rehabilitation, following the removal of plaster from my legs in the first instance, and from my body in the second period of recovery. It was a case of tough love. When you have been encased in plaster for weeks or months, your limbs become used to being immobile. Your muscles are seriously out of condition. Just the simple act of sitting up after being on your back for months can be a dizzying experience.

I have memory of excruciating pain, and muscles seemingly turned to elastic after daily knee flexion exercises. Step by small step, however, I began to shuffle down corridors, using a walking frame or crutches.

Special thanks are due to my strict yet patient physios, whose work is often measured in small victories over long lengths of time.

Homeward Bound

Eventually, my physical progress enabled me to return home. Saying goodbye to faithful residents and staff at the hostel was a bittersweet experience. I swallowed a lump in my throat, hearing a resident sobbing in the bathroom as I left. Still, my return to the family fold was indescribably delicious. Seeing our home for the first time in months lifted my heart. I was nervous, though, about physically coping with new routines at home. My parents' practical reassurance helped me to adjust.

A gift of goldfish from my Sunday school class added excitement to the joyful welcome. This act of thoughtful generosity was inspired by a Bible memory verse from Galatians. I was to call one of the three fish "Galatia." Why? To help me remember the epistle's message: "Therefore, as we have opportunity, let us do good to all people, especially to those who belong to the family of believers" (Gal. 6:10 NIV).

After the six-month recovery from surgery and rehabilitation on my knees, my orthopaedic surgeon announced in a matter-of-fact tone, "The operation didn't work, did it?" His pronouncement was no surprise, but his words made the result sound more final. My knees were still bent. A visiting American surgeon consulted on my case, saying that he would have approached the knee surgery a different way.

Ever since, I have hated the idea of surgery. I realised to my sorrow the limitations of the medical professions. To this day, although I have the kindest and most thorough of Christian general practitioners, I struggle going to doctors. They do their best, but magic wands seem to be out of stock when it comes to management of adult cerebral palsy. However, I am grateful that their non-surgical interventions enable me to be as well as I can.

Despite the big disappointment of the knee surgery results, I believe that the rehabilitation process for my knees and hip was a great learning experience, increasing my exposure to residents and staff working in the disability field.

5

The Agony and The Ecstasy

Northbridge, Sydney, New South Wales
High School—Spastic Centre

FOLLOWING THESE OPERATIONS, my ability to walk from class to class, necessary in mainstream secondary education, was limited. In that era, there was only spasmodic awareness of the need to improve wheelchair access in regular educational facilities. Hence, the decision was made for me to go to the special school attached to the Spastic Centre. Extensive mobility was not required there. The logistics involved in this kind of education, though, meant the family moved to nearby Northbridge, where Dad took up a new parish.

My high school education routine took the shape of a bus collecting me from home each school day. The burly bus drivers lifted me from my wheelchair into a bus seat, ready for the rattling ride to school along with my fellow passengers who had been picked up before me. The situation was reversed at day's end.

This experience opened my eyes further to the wide variety of manifestations of disability, even within the one subgroup of cerebral palsy. In my class of about fourteen, there were pupils with unsteady gait, speech difficulties, involuntary spasms, and facial tics. Students who had little or no hand function used electric typewriters with the help of a strapped headpiece, on which was attached a long pointer. They used the pointer to hammer letters and words with their bobbing heads.

However, we were not simply a conglomeration of medical conditions. It was no surprise that there were vast differences in personality too. There were young men with aristocratic bearing, footy-mad girls, teenagers with leadership skills and giant determination, adolescents from lower socio-economic backgrounds, chatty friend-makers, great intellects, and some with considerable grace and kindness. A few originated from a different cultural tradition. Others lacked social confidence, but compensated with a wonderful sense of humour.

Schoolwork through the Correspondence School at Kings Cross was predominantly done in the mornings, with occupational and physiotherapy sessions in the afternoons. Each of us worked at a different level of high school. We were supervised by a dignified high school teacher of senior age, assisted by a teacher's aide. Part of their responsibilities was to be our amanuenses. We dictated our thoughts as they wrote them in a book. We would then transcribe our own words via the electric typewriter. I wonder whether this process was designed to encourage verbal expression.

Wider Links and Obligations

Medical students visited us in the classroom weekly to discuss our lifestyles and education experiences. There were a mixture of engaged students who listened well, and those who were bored and only there to tick an educational box.

Our links with other community representatives were further strengthened by presentations on road safety by police, and weekly religious education.

Therapy and Daily Living

In return for voluntary work undertaken by Mum and Dad for the centre, I had access to therapy sessions. A speech therapist led us in group discussions on current affairs. Outlining the importance of celebrating small triumphs, she once told the story of a small boy with cerebral palsy painstakingly learning to gain enough breath control to blow out his birthday candles. I realised I took many things for granted. Further, I believe speech therapy was given to compensate us, as correspondence school students, for the lack of classroom discussion normally available to students in mainstream schools.

Physiotherapy consisted of exercises and extensive walks on my Canadian crutches through the winding corridors and up long flights of stairs. I believe this period enabled me to be the fittest that I ever was or was to become.

Occupational therapy concentrated on encouraging independent living skills. Specially designed assistive equipment like plastic stocking gutters and long-handled shoehorns helped me to dress independently, albeit very slowly. I learned how to dress differently because, due to surgery, I could not bend in the middle well to tie shoelaces or put on stockings.

The daily dressing ritual became a continuing aggravation because it took so much energy and time to complete. I was often tired before the day started, because I had to get up with the birds to compensate for my slowness. My frustration reminds me of a story of unknown origin, of a little boy learning how to tie his shoelaces. He started to cry. When his mum asked what the matter was, he wailed, "I will have to tie my shoelaces for the rest of my life!"

How did I remain sane during this mind-deadening daily routine of making myself presentable? For a time I incorporated my Christian meditation practice with dressing, recalling Paul's words about putting on the armour of God: "Therefore put on the full armour of God, so that when the day of evil comes, you may be able to stand your ground, and after you have done everything, to stand. Stand firm then, with the belt of truth buckled around your waist, with the breastplate of righteousness in place, and with your feet fitted with the readiness that comes from the gospel of peace" (Eph. 6:13–15 NIV).

These were dramatic words indeed to wage war on my dressing routine. However, in later years, I was grateful for the speedy assistance of good-humoured carers. Their cheery chatter lured me from grumpy morning sluggishness to the hope of a new day. Is it my delusion of aristocratic grandeur that encourages me to think they are now my fabulous ladies-in-waiting?

Occasionally I was privileged to have a capable male carer to assist me with dressing. The service organisation failed to inform me that I was allocated to him, though. When he arrived at the door, I greeted him in my birthday suit. Embarrassed, for a split second I thought he was the plumber!

I pay tribute to this great army of people who lubricate the wheels of my existence with skill and respect. Some carers love children's literature; others have family experience of disability. Some tell of online dating experiences, deaths of loved ones, and care of canines. Our conversations range far and wide, from grief-laden words to hilarious comedy routines.

Correspondence School Education

Let's talk about the process of correspondence education in the setting of self-paced work in the classroom. Each of us was sent a big package of reading material suitable for our academic level and subject. The copious information was complemented by numerous questions and longer assignments, which we were obliged to complete and send back to our subject teachers for correction. Their comments, red ticks, and crosses then arrived for our perusal, accompanying our next bundle of work.

Black-and-white TV was a useful means of making up for the oral teaching deficits of correspondence education. I remember watching TV science experiments. In our classroom, we watched the biggest scientific experiment to date—the first landing on the moon by Neil Armstrong. We held our breaths as we watched his first steps onto the crater-like surface. I prayed that he did not blow up.

Learning French conversation by correspondence was also difficult. I tried to improve my French conversation by watching simple French stories on TV. Recording French conversation on reel-to-reel tape recorders and sending the tapes back by mail to the correspondence teachers was another requirement. Giving feedback on my feeble attempts at the French accent, my teacher suggested I place a peg on my nose to improve my imitation of the nasalised quality of the language. I didn't oblige.

I missed oral communication in class discussion, but correspondence education helped me in my written skills. I caused Dad some hilarity by mispronouncing words that I had never heard spoken. For example, I pronounced *hyperbole* "hypa-BOWL." The correct pronunciation, of course, is "hy-PER-bo-lee."

I relished the subjects of English and modern history. On one occasion, I wrote an essay on the causes of World War II while watching a TV movie, *Nicholas and Alexandra* (not my usual practice). It was the only essay I ever wrote in my life for which I received full marks. I was shocked. Perhaps my brain works better in a relaxed state.

Unfortunately, I had to be heavily bribed with chocolate as I trudged through dry accounts of the Peloponnesian Wars in ancient history. The thick textbook with miniscule print and a boring grey cover did nothing to convince me of the relevance of the comparative military might of Athens and Sparta to my small adolescent life.

My skill in maths plummeted in high school. High marks had been common for me in primary school, but I failed maths in my trial higher school certificate (HSC). I scraped in for the final big public exam. Algebra and logarithms made little sense to me.

My second-to-last year at school, between the two public exams, was marked by low motivation. I grew to hate the drudgery. My pace of work slowed right down. Correspondence teachers wrote to my folks, unbeknown to me, saying that if I didn't speed up my work, I would not be able to sit for my HSC. They sent me extra reading before exams to help me catch up.

Furious arguments with my folks occasionally bubbled with great energy in the cauldron of my adolescent witchery. Heated conversations were usually about me wanting to leave school. My parents would not let me. Like all teenagers, I thought they were mean and lacked understanding. With the benefit of hindsight, I am glad they did not surrender to the whims of their recalcitrant rebel. Tedious though it was at the time, I now realise that gaining my HSC widened my career options as a person with a disability. Such a milestone was another string to my bow as I did battle with future barriers of discrimination in the open employment market.

The reward of wrestling about my educational future crystallised later. I recall a state of sheer ecstasy after completing my *very* last HSC exam ever. No other exams I took before or since had so much pressure associated with them. My future direction depended on good results. I had strained towards this finish line, and now the tension released in my body like sputtering air in a deflating balloon.

Nevertheless, my last day of school at the Spastic Centre was surprisingly tinged with sadness. I looked back at the entrance of the school through the bus window as the vehicle rumbled down the ramp towards home for the very last time. I was assaulted with a sense of nostalgia. The protective bubble of security was bursting. There would no longer be staff around to hover, waiting to pick me up when I fell. I was not likely to see my friends from this circle again. Who knew what the future held?

A mixture of excitement and anxiety coursed through my veins. I was on the cusp of danger on the one hand and possibility on the other.

Waiting for the Next Leap

During our holidays, HSC results arrived by post. We rang Ernie, postman at our home post office, to read out the grades over the phone. The marks were much better than I expected or, at one stage, deserved. Communication methods from the Education Department have changed dramatically with the digital era. Not many people now can boast that their postie passed on this happy news by phone.

My English teacher informed me that my marks were high enough for university. Her encouragement, I believe, was God's provision. If she had not rung, I would not have attempted tertiary education. I cannot stress enough the importance of my teacher's belief in me. She took the time to give me hope, thereby changing my career direction.

Around this period, Mum and I navigated our way to a pokey office to complete a vocational guidance test. Two incidents stand out in my mind. I asked the vocational counsellor, much to my mother's embarrassment, "Do you think I will ever marry?"

To the counsellor's credit, he did not laugh, taking the enquiry seriously. However, whatever brownie points he gained in my estimation for tackling that difficult question, he slid down in my eighteen-year-old judgement when, after perusing my results, he said, "You are not university material. You need a job with high social contact. You would be good at showing people where the toilets are!" My self-esteem also took a tumble.

However, he galvanised my sheer determination to prove a professional's predictions wrong, stubborn mule that I am. It is true that during careers in social welfare, librarianship, and chaplaincy, I directed numerous people to restrooms, but I am thankful to God that my brain and heart were challenged beyond those simple requirements.

Recreation in My Teens

Learning to Swim

One of the joys of my teen years was learning to swim with an amiable World War II veteran who was a single amputee. My parents took me faithfully to the pool where he taught kids with disability to swim.

On one occasion, a girl with a severe visual impairment stood upright at the edge of the pool, looking very nervous. Our instructor called out to her in his encouraging voice while waist deep in the pool, "Jump in. I'll be here." A mighty splash marked the diving milestone for the plucky girl. How brave she was to dive into dark nothingness for the first time. An exercise of trust in her teacher was rewarded by spectators' thunderous applause.

While learning breaststroke and modified backstroke, I relished an equally special experience—feeling weightless. Buoyed by water, I could walk unaided. My exuberance was heightened because normal movement on land in a disabled body is such a high-effort endeavour. I wish I could be surrounded by an ever-present big puddle of water on land.

Girl Guides

Joining the Girl Guides was a window opening to practical education. Each week our Guide leader and volunteers arrived at the Spastic Centre. As high school girls, my classmates and I engaged in activities specially geared for people with disability. We listened to lectures on first aid, health, safety, survival, and brain development skills. In addition, we learned and tested for specific badges in skills such as needlework, health, hospitality, and creative writing. Some of us attended camps, occasionally in tents, where we learned skills like building a campfire and square-lashing.

I remember being part of an international Girl Guide jamboree in Sydney, where Guides gathered to celebrate the spirit and skill of the movement. We were honoured to meet Lady Baden-Powell, who, as widow of the founder of the Scout movement, personally greeted our extension company. On another occasion, I sat with my eyes glued on Princess Margaret, the Queen's sister, as she attended a Guide function.

There were two other local highlights in guiding. The first was the joyful wedding of our Guide captain, which Dad conducted at our church. Her Guide company formed a proud guard of honour following the ceremony, smartly attired in our pale blue uniforms and bright yellow ties. The presentation of my Queen's Guide certificate on the lawns of New South Wales Government House by the governor was a second memorable occasion. The festivity crowned the hard work required in preparing for badges of all descriptions. The practical education and friendship I gained in these years complemented the academic slant of the correspondence school.

Uniting Church Youth Group

How can I describe the significance of the Northbridge Uniting Church Youth Group in my young life? It was a forum for searching religious discussions and a great avenue of service and leadership opportunities. The members offered warm friendship and accepted me for who I was. Relationships were the focus, not my disability.

I enthusiastically joined fundraising fun runs, at the mercy of puffing pushers of my wheelchair who pounded across Sydney Harbour Bridge. On another nail-biting occasion, four strapping young men stepped very carefully across jagged rocks and lifted my wheelchair (with me in it!) along the top of the majestic Bridal Veil Falls in the Blue Mountains. The concentration and teamwork required were remarkable. The view, a long way below in the cavernous valley, was spectacular, with green eucalypt treetops swaying in the gentle breeze. One missed step would have meant we were cactus. I am glad our parents were blissfully unaware of the risk at the time, but the adrenaline rush was worth every second. The thrill of those moments has stayed with me for nearly forty years. The incident also showed to me the extent to which wonderful friends would go to include me in their outdoor activities.

For all its youthful exuberance, one of our group's strengths was its developing social conscience. Our activities included escorting a teenage boy from a children's home on picnics, sleeping in dorms to the sounds of thunderous snores during church camps, hosting people with intellectual disabilities, and building houses (under supervision) for disadvantaged people at Christian work camps. Running coffee-shop nights with live bands were ear-splitting attempts at youth outreach.

Once I had the opportunity to attend a district church youth camp. The only glitch was that I would be required to sleep on the floor in a tent. As I mentally prepared myself for the event, I visualised strangers having to transfer me from my wheelchair to the ground. If I needed to go to the bathroom at night, I would have to wake up a few people to complete heave-ho duty.

As the time approached, I became more anxious and filled with dread. I had no doubt of the willingness of young and able-bodied fellow Christians to assist me, but I had not yet met some of them.

I shared my concerns with Dad. He asked me, "Why do you want to go to camp?"

I realised the only reason I wanted to go was to prove to myself that I could surmount any obstacle, even if it killed me. Enjoyment and friendship were not even on my agenda. What a misdirected motivation! I decided not to go—a resolution which was surprisingly freeing. Rather than experiencing defeat, I discovered that I did not have to win all battles. Choosing worthwhile challenges with a productive end in mind is completely different. One does not have to climb to Mt Everest just because it is there!

Deep friendships formed within our youth group. Who could forget Tim, a genuine, intelligent young man with a heart of gold? We enjoyed hitching lifts with him in his blue VW van. He could be fun-loving and high-spirited on occasions, and was a valued mate.

When Tim began his university studies, it took him a while to find his niche. He switched his course preferences several times. Over time, despite the affection in which he was held, he became withdrawn from us. In our lounge room, I remember him sitting on the settee, seemingly deep in thought. But he was not able to engage in social conversation any more. Instead, he made inappropriate, soft hissing sounds interrupted by self-conscious giggles. We did not know what to make of these unexpected developments. We continued to include him in our activities, but it became a strain for him and a puzzle to us.

He was admitted by his family to a private psychiatric clinic for a while. My last memory of Tim, after he returned home, is of him at the wheel of his van, driving us to a picnic. He seemed to be the relaxed Tim of old, laughing and joining in jokes. It was good to have our old friend back, or so we thought.

Imagine our jaw-dropping horror when, a few days later, his parents notified us that Tim had committed suicide. We were speechless. It seemed that our affection for him was not enough to support him through his tormented valleys. I have since discovered that he had been diagnosed with schizophrenia. We also learned that before a suicide attempt, a person may show outward signs of happiness, because they are relieved to have made a final decision to end their lives.

Tim's choice to cut short his life had a dramatic effect on us all. We were a caring group, but we were assaulted with feelings of guilt. What more could we have done to prevent this? Why? Why? Why? There were a thousand "if onlys" which tumbled around our heads.

All I can say is there are no easy answers in the tragedy of a young life cut short. It was not only difficult for his mates, but heart-rending for his family too. Sometimes love is not enough to assuage a friend's deep turmoil. It took me a long time to process that, despite our best efforts to reach out to him, it was ultimately Tim's choice to end his suffering in the way he did.

We still remember you with deep affection, Tim, our gentle giant, even after forty years have elapsed.

Northbridge Church Life

As in most churches, there were many faith strands within our congregation. Among them were scholars and university professors who appreciated the depth of sermon preparation and reflection which Dad offered.

A strong charismatic influence also held sway. The concept of baptism of the Holy Spirit assumed great importance for some. Occasionally,

I felt like a second-class Christian if I didn't express my faith with the same exuberance or with the added bonus of speaking in tongues. In fact, I sensed, rightly or wrongly, that in the eyes of dedicated followers, I didn't quite make the grade.

Coupled with the charismatic movement, a strong Evangelical influence permeated the spirits of others. One lady, I am sure with the best of intentions, asked me frequently, "Is the Lord blessing you?" In the midst of adolescent turmoil, I was uncomfortable in answering such a direct question. There were times during that dark period that I thought God was not blessing me.

Looking back with the benefit of life experience, I now appreciate the strengths and limitations of different faith expressions. What I am sensitive to is that our Christian spirituality, precious though it is, should not be imposed on others in a domineering manner.

At one point, a keen Bible class leader assumed teaching responsibility for my peers and me. With her broad Bible knowledge and deep evangelical faith, her dedicated care for her teenage pupils was second to none. I am grateful for the solid grounding she gave us in the Christian life.

Despite her wonderful qualities, our teacher was an intense personality. Nursing my anxious teenage mind and stomach, I occasionally shuffled off to her class with a Bible in one hand and an antacid tablet in the other. What a tricky, conflicted combination for mature Christian growth!

I sometimes erroneously interpreted her strict moral principles. This led me to become legalistic in my judgements of others who did not match up to what I thought was right. Dad warned that I was becoming Pharisee-like in my assessment of people. "Compassionate understanding of people with all their foibles is at the heart of our relationships," he suggested.

A lasting fruit of our leader's teaching was her encouragement to confirm our faith in Jesus Christ and offer service to church and community. The special service of commitment was enhanced with beautiful white flowers and inspiring organ music. Nature and melody nodded their approval as we made our vows to God.

Little by little, I arrived at a more restful, less judgemental place of faith. I struggled with some overzealous Christians who wanted to possess my soul with both hands. This was at the time when charismatic renewal was in full force. Some devotees of the movement were anxious that I be baptised in the Holy Spirit and speak in tongues. Despite attempts to lead me into this experience, it did not work for me. I felt a religious failure.

Dad helped me understand that speaking in tongues was only one of the gifts of the Spirit, and that love was the greatest quality. He mentioned one of the motherly saints of the local church to help me see that her living faith was as legitimate as that of the more openly fervent members. To me, she was the epitome of Christian grace and humour. She did not freely use the name of God in ordinary conversations. Yet her genuine expression of faith was evident in her understanding and compassion. The words of Jesus, "Thus, you will know them by their fruits," oozed comfort (Matt. 7:20 NRSV).

I realise now that no one of us has a monopoly on all truth about God. Each may well have a glimpse of understanding. In sharing our insights into the nature of faith, it is important not use our understanding of religion as a weapon to manipulate others. Rather, following the Spirit of the compassionate Christ, we need to lovingly create a place of safety, where the meaning of life can be explored without judgement. In this space, we can, together, experience the mystery of God.

On one occasion, Dad asked the young people to suggest sermon topics for evening services. When I gathered courage, I asked him to preach on "When God seems far away." This choice was probably an accurate reflection of what I was feeling in the midst of my adolescent angst. With his usual pastoral sensitivity, Dad announced, "Don't worry for the moment about what you find difficult to believe in. Hold fast to that which you now know to be true." The prayer-laden words of the anguished father of a boy with epilepsy in Jesus's time gave me hope: "I do believe; help me overcome my unbelief!" (Mark 9:23–25 NIV). Jesus was particularly responsive to such an honest, heartfelt cry.

Trials of Adolescence

My tumultuous teenage hormones raged. I didn't know how to control them. I had the usual adolescent uncertainties about friendships, romance, the meaning of life, and depression. I experienced confusion about the validity of different Christian expressions. I felt the absence of God at times.

The battle inside me also centred round conflict between "normal" independence, which all teenagers try to assert, and my necessary dependence on parents and others for everyday needs because of my physical condition. I often worried about whether I would be able to live independently in a flat, either on my own or with others. I often cried uncontrollably at the difficulties of disability and my dislike of school.

Such conflicts reached an agonised climax one night when I sobbed out the words, "I wish I had never been born!" Embarrassed Dad, who valued dignity and self-containment, firmly closed the bedroom window to stop my screams of anguish from reaching the ears of the next-door neighbours. I am sure my parents just didn't know how to cope with the monster that was growing before their eyes.

I remember that they coped with strictness, admonishing me for being disrespectful and self-centred—which I was, undoubtedly. But at that moment, the horror of being me was overwhelming. I just wanted to be understood. I am sure they were as confused as I was. They deserved medals of valour.

Later I noticed there was a paperback addition to Dad's laden book-shelves, the title of which was something to the effect of *How to Survive Your Teenager's Adolescence.*

I don't quite know how we navigated those turbulent waves. All I know was that my parents and Mal were steadfast in their loyalty. I had stable friends. Believe it or not, reading empathic books by Swiss Christian psychiatrist Paul Tournier was great therapy at this time. His insights into the human condition, warts and all, nurtured my bleeding soul. As a result of that healing experience, I have become a firm believer in the power of what is called bibliotherapy—prescribing appropriate books to meet particular life challenges.

Discerning Vocational Choices

I am deeply drawn to Frederick Buechner's definition of the meaning of the word *vocation*: "The place God calls you is the place where your deep gladness and the world's deep hunger meet."[1] Discerning those gifts as one grows up requires trial and error.

Like able-bods, as I grew up I dreamed about what I wanted to be. It became like trying on different styles of clothes to see if they fitted. As a young girl, I wanted to be a hairdresser, a vet, a secretary, and yes, even an obstetrician. (I must have had a rather romanticised view of babies at the time!) I thought about becoming a medical records librarian, a lab technician, a social worker, a speech therapist, or an elocutionist. I take my hat off to my parents, who patiently listened to my wildest dreams. Often my choices were made on the basis of the careers of role models I admired at the time. My parents tried to remain hopeful while pointing out the realistic factors that inevitably need to be considered when living with a moderate to severe physical disability.

So began a search for meaningful direction. At one stage, the possibility of becoming a deaconess (a female church leader) lit a flame in my heart. Dad and I made enquiries. We discovered that candidates were required to have previous work experience before launching into a religious vocation.

During the post-school, pre-university period, I spent a trial few days at a sheltered workshop, Centre Industries, administered by the Spastic Centre. They offered a variety of employment options for candidates to gain work experience. Factory work, assembling pieces of a switchboard, was repetitive. The clerical option held more promise, but I didn't believe it was intellectually satisfying. The only pleasant event which lifted my spirits was a short-lived, one-way crush on a dishy-looking, blond, able-bodied supervisor. Be still my beating heart!

Macquarie University

With the encouragement of my English teacher ringing in my ears, I listed my preferences for university study. I had a leaning towards psychology, thinking that would lead me eventually into a welfare profession. The new Macquarie University, which accepted me for enrolment, was close to home, offered behavioural sciences as a discipline, and was relatively wheelchair accessible.

My course was funded by the Commonwealth Government Rehabilitation Scheme—a package which opened the future for me like a blossoming flower. It granted me opportunities that ordinarily my parents could not afford, much less I on my own. It is fashionable to criticise government, but during that period, my funded university education, coupled with an intense rehabilitation programme, gave me wings to fly into the future.

Included in this educational assistance was government-supported transport to and from university, until I obtained my driver's licence.

Hire cars or taxis arrived at my door to escort me. Once, an old, shiny, black Rolls Royce appeared, when no other car was available. Our middle-class family blushed at the sight of such luxury. Their discomfort was lessened a little by the car's courteous driver. I practised my royal wave cheekily as the car moved away from the kerb! Mum and Dad slinked away before neighbours could see.

I learned much from these drivers. I was asked on a date by one who had never seen me before. I politely declined. Another recently bereaved driver poured out his heart to me, sharing his deep love for his departed wife. Sometimes the taxi became a confessional. Even at a young age I developed a deep respect for people's stories of suffering.

Other drivers, who were curious about my disability, began our conversations even before greeting me. The first question in those cases was always "What's wrong with you?" Despite finding this direct approach confrontational, I answered honestly, in the hope that it deepened their understanding of disability. In an ideal world, I would have preferred that they establish a relationship with me before launching into a personal discussion.

Frequently, I hitched a lift with other students in their cars. The opportunity for light-hearted banter with people my age was a great boon. We complained about essay topics, regretted tight deadlines, and joked about the absurdities of campus life.

Transport aside, my formal learning was also a rich opportunity. Tertiary education opened my horizons—not just to the written word, but to classroom discussion, an experience not developed during my time in correspondence school. In a first-year psychology tutorial, some members of the class were hypnotised as an experiment. Unfortunately, I was not one of the successful subjects, but it was great fun nonetheless.

I soaked up Reformation history like a sponge. Martin Luther, the German Protestant reformer of the sixteenth century, quickly became one of my heroes, partly because I sensed a strong connection between his intense personal struggle and mine. No matter how hard he tried, he felt he could never win God's approval. Neither saying the Mass correctly nor confessing all his minute sins did the trick. He still sensed his unworthiness, until he plumbed the depths of the beauty of the Scripture: "For by grace you have been saved through faith, and this is not your own doing; it is the gift of God—not the result of works, so that no one may boast" (Eph. 2:8–9 NRSV).

The insight, that being saved was nothing to do with personal effort to please God but simply a reliance on the merciful gift of the Creator, liberated Luther from a life of anxious perfectionism.

What was the personal application for me? There is nothing I can do to earn God's approval. His mercy is sheer gift. My acts of service are simply a free response to gracious favour, not ends in themselves. My own tussle to reach perfection in an imperfect body was on its way to being resolved.

Later, I realised that Jesus's injunction to "be perfect" was based on a Greek word *teleios*. Matt. 5:48). William Barclay, a Scottish New Testament scholar, suggests that "a thing is perfect if it fully realises the purpose for which it was made"[2] The context for Jesus's words relates to loving others, just as God loves. So living out my purpose in life involves impartial looking out for the welfare of others, regardless of whether I happen to "like" them or not.

In other psychology and sociology courses, I was exposed to smatterings of Marxism, feminism, and behavioural psychology. We conducted and wrote up our own psychological experiments. My strong interests were in personality development and psychopathology. I was intrigued with a group visit we did to a psychiatric facility. We interviewed a young child who had been in a sexually abusive situation, a man who had had a long-term battle with alcohol, and an older man who allegedly had murdered a family member. These experiences added depth to my understanding of the human condition.

I was still in a manual wheelchair at the time, so wheeling myself from one end of the campus to another, up and down steep ramps, was exhausting. Friends and strangers alike offered to push me at least some of the way to lectures, which was a relief. The university counsellor was an astute, caring individual. He formed a group of Macquarie students with disabilities to advise him on physical access issues and other difficulties.

One such unexpected challenge presented itself early in my campus days. Careering down a ramp towards glass doors, my hair flying, I dropped my unsecured briefcase and capsized into an earthy mound. I had grass stains on my clothes to prove it. A lecturer, his eyes as big as saucers, witnessed the event from his top-storey window. He ran down to rescue me. Were there any limits to the lengths I would go to attract attention?

My ever-practical mum then designed thick strings which connected from each side of my briefcase handle to the metal struts already on my wheelchair. Life was a lot safer from then on.

Socialising with friends was an enjoyable part of university life. I have fond memories of laughter as we shared lunch and conversation, lounging on sun-drenched lawns. I also joined the Evangelical Union, a campus group. Attending lectures by Christian speakers stretched my brain as I sought to integrate intellect and faith.

Taking the plunge, I volunteered in the friendly office of Willoughby Council Community Aid Centre over the university break. Filing and answering welfare enquiries added to my experience of the big, wide world.

Mt Wilga Rehabilitation Centre

While studying part-time at Macquarie in my first year, I attended a year-long programme at Mt Wilga Rehabilitation Centre.

Physiotherapy, vocational training, typing, and driver education were the main items on the agenda.

Having realised that driving a car normally, with foot pedals, was out of the question, I began my formal driving instruction at the rehabilitation centre—a scary adventure. Shorty was my instructor. He was forthright in his communication. With sweaty palms, I trembled during lessons around the streets in a car with hand-controls. In those initial driving experiences, he pronounced with characteristic honesty, "You drive like Mrs Murphy's knitting." Many a time I arrived home as a nervous wreck. As a gal who rarely drank tea or coffee, I begged Mum for two cups of tea laced with sugar. There was great celebration when I passed my driving test on the first go!

I met rehabilitation clients who opened my eyes to the breadth of human suffering. Frustrated young men with spinal cord injuries, rehabilitating after traumatic motorbike accidents, grieved strongly for their loss of youthful physical prowess. These raw conversations were enough to make me to anti-motorbikes for a while.

Another memorable encounter with a physio client opened my eyes to others' challenges. Because of a traumatic brain injury, a thirty-year-old woman could not remember any events prior to and including her twenty-first birthday. How sad! Memory, I discovered, is crucial for forming our identities, roots, and history. It helps to make sense of who we are and to whom we belong.

Unemployment

After the intellectual freedom at Macquarie University, I graduated with a Bachelor of Arts degree. Who could forget the feeling of exultation I felt as I wore my black academic gown with golden hood and mortarboard? I felt suitably spruce as I was presented to the vice chancellor to receive my degree. After the ceremony, he pushed my wheelchair with due decorum down the aisle.

The unmistakable joy of achievement was soon tempered by the crushing experience of eight months of unemployment. Depression and a sense of a lack of meaning became my constant companions. I grew tired of devouring newspapers, circling job ads, typing applications, and waiting endlessly for the rejection letters and the follow-up phone calls. By nature, I was not one to blow my own trumpet, and yet that was the game I felt I had to play to get a foot in the door. Kind friends asked, "Have you found a job yet?" My continuing "No" seemed to hammer failure into my heart.

One phone conversation I had with a prospective employer was memorable. I listed some of my qualities and qualifications. He said, "You don't seem to have a lot of confidence, do you?" Constant rejection played havoc with my sense of worth. His comment, though truthful, did not help.

Another curly knot I tried to disentangle was the inevitable cry of employers: "We need experience!"

My question was "How do you gain work experience when you aren't even given access to the job market?"

My personal struggle was set against a backdrop of relatively high unemployment in Australia. Competition for jobs was rife. One public service job for which I applied had five hundred applicants. One of the few interviews I was granted was for a public service job in the Stamp Duty Office. I was not granted the position, but the nature of the task required did not light a fire in my soul. Perhaps that showed, despite my best effort.

A dilemma continually raised its head for me—whether to disclose my disability in an application or not. I always did, because I thought it would reflect on my integrity if I was granted an interview and they were shocked. Prospective employers might ask themselves, "What else is she hiding from us?"

If I could have found a great cosmic purpose for this agonising hiatus, then unemployment might have been easier to bear. At the time, I found none.

Hospitality at Home

During this trying time, my experience of a wide variety of people broadened as our hospitable Northbridge household welcomed people from overseas. Dad had moved from being a parish minister to a mission administrator with a Uniting Church agency. Part of his role was to provide friendly shelter to visiting mission workers.

I remember a conversation we had with two indigenous Papua and New Guinea men. They, along with us, were watching an old episode of *Rin Tin Tin* on TV. As was a regular custom in these old black-and-white programmes, the Native American population was sadly being annihilated by the US Cavalry. We, as seasoned watchers, had become desensitised to what was happening. Our visitors, however, became most distressed. Upon enquiry, we discovered that they believed that the scenario was real. They thought that Native American actors were in reality being slaughtered for the sake of our light entertainment. What things do we take for granted?

Another visitor we welcomed was a Uniting Church worker from Darwin, Northern Territory. Cyclone Tracy had wreaked havoc over his city and house, resulting also in the heart-rending loss of his wife as she was caught under rubble. I cannot imagine what grief was going through his mind.

A young New Zealand mission worker, toiling in an Aboriginal community on the northern tip of Australia, also came to us for some R & R after a strenuous time. He was only a few years older than Mal and me. We struck up a deep, lifelong friendship. He eventually married one of the local girls after he became involved in our close-knit youth group.

University of New South Wales

Back on the unemployment front, finally a new direction in my life became clearer. The employment office with which I had connected suggested a more vocationally oriented course. My arts degree was too generic. I investigated completing a social work degree, but the university administration did not recognise most of my prior educational credits. To follow this track would mean a further three years at university. A year's graduate diploma in librarianship seemed a better possibility.

After being accepted into the course, I waged a heroic battle each day. Driving in peak hour across the huge Sydney Harbour Bridge was only the beginning. I felt as if I had to breathe in to fit into its narrow lanes. There was no margin for error.

Wheelchair access on this far-flung, impersonal campus was difficult, further exacerbated by the fact that the school of librarianship was at opposite end of the grounds from the library itself. The geography was Everest-like in its mountainous terrain. Using my car to traverse distances entailed energy, coaxing my tired legs in and out of the driver's seat and assembling my wheelchair. The workload mirrored the steep physical inclines. My physical and mental endurance was severely tested, especially when I had to negotiate long distances for back-to-back commitments.

One senior lecturer put the stuffing back into my wavering heart with the words, "You are very resilient, my dear." Such encouragement is a vital, underrated quality. At times I was sorely tempted to give up. However, minute by minute, hour by hour, day by day, I kept plugging, because the prospect of unemployment was horrific. The ambivalent, yet ultimately positive words of Samuel Beckett, the Irish novelist, seem apt here: "You must go on, I can't go on, … I'll go on."[3]

During this time, I uncovered an unexpected passion. I was required to complete a thesis on bibliotherapy. This branch of knowledge, on the cusp of art and science, is the therapeutic skill of selecting books for clients to read in light of their specific challenges. More specifically, material (whether written or audiovisual) can be chosen for clients with physical, intellectual, and/or psychiatric disabilities in psychological, relational, or communal situations.

This fascinating subject gripped my interest in an otherwise strenuous time. No doubt, the power of this health-giving tool had been planted and hidden in my literary heart in earlier years, although at that time I had no name for it. An inspiring book or film can indeed put wind under flagging wings.

The librarianship course itself was my gateway to a first career. Friendly staff and students collaborated to arrange frequent visits for me to different kinds of research centres—public libraries, children's libraries, schools, and universities. We browsed through the collections and ferreted through organisational structures of specialist libraries too, such as collections in the fields of music and building. Obviously it was difficult for me to determine what kind of library I would enjoy working in, but my tendencies were towards special or university libraries.

University of New South Wales Law Library

A gentle ex–Catholic priest, as head librarian of the law library, gave me my first paid job ever. The six-hour-a-week casual employment was a thrilling milestone. When I tried to explain to him how much it meant to me, he acted as if it was the most natural thing in the world to offer a librarianship student a part-time job. Gold stars for him!

NSW Council of Social Services Library

After graduating from my course, I became a volunteer library assistant in the small library of the New South Wales Council of Social Services. I was able to get a foot in the door through the efforts of a dynamic friend who had a disability himself. Finger-clawing experience had taught me that it was helpful to volunteer to expand my networks of people and to gain valuable job skills.

I was exposed to a competent, no-nonsense, feminist boss who was an ardent lobbyist for better conditions in the social service sector. This was a useful education in itself for one who had been somewhat protected from different world views. With the benefit of more life experience now, I no longer consider my Christian journey a safe haven, hidden away from the complexities of the world. Instead, my faith encourages me to launch outside my comfort zone. Faith now challenges me to ask continuous questions, such as "Where is God working in this situation and through these people?" Nevertheless, at that time, my exposure to philosophies outside the academic environment was indeed expanding.

Through my association with the library, I met a project officer with Australian Council for Rehabilitation of Disabled (ACROD), a national lobby and advocacy organisation. The researcher was exploring the difficulties faced by people with disability. She asked me what my particular challenges were. Some weeks later, through her advocacy, I was offered a post as a paid library assistant for her organisation. Wonder of wonders, my feet were a-tapping!

With this chest-expanding news under my belt, I returned home with suppressed excitement, barely containing the bubbling energy inside me. When there was a gap in the mealtime conversation, I proclaimed with metaphorical trumpet in hand, "By the way, I got a paid job today."

The family, who had been with me through the spikes and dips of anticipation and disappointment of job hunting, hugged me warmly, amid the inevitable oohs and aahs. "Who, why, and how" questions tumbled out.

ACROD Sydney Library

ACROD Sydney Library was housed in a pokey room in a building that was antique, even Dickensian in quality. Information was predominantly stored in book or article form. Its subject matter obviously covered disabilities of all descriptions, together with issues relating to access, employment, education, family support, income security, government policy and statistics, welfare services, and housing, as well as the psychological and sociological aspects of disability.

Our clientele were researchers, policymakers, family members, special education teachers, students, and people with disability. Prior to the advent of email, requests for assistance arrived via letter and phone with the occasional drop-in visitor. I worked part-time in tandem with two other part-time women. With their guidance, I was fortunate to learn more about the disability scene beyond the limited horizons of my experience. Apart from the enjoyment I received from people contact and the opportunity to soak up knowledge, I thoroughly enjoyed attending national conferences. Here, experts in the disability field gathered to cross-fertilise ideas. I also was happy to offer feedback and ideas on various projects, including wheelchair design.

The words of a dynamic ACROD director in my early years still make an impression on me: "Don't always accept the status quo." Her philosophy marked the beginning of my long journey to realise that I, teamed up with others, could influence others to change things in the community for the better. In the past, I had been encouraged to accept things as they were. This is a helpful strategy in many scenarios. However, her ethos opened the doors of my thinking. Great things happen if people of good will plan well and push with the energy of many.

I became aware that ACROD planned to move its headquarters to Canberra, the nation's capital. This placed the organisation in a better position to lobby the government. While it was a strategic move for them, it forced me to contemplate a future away from home for the first time. My dread of further unemployment if I stayed in the Sydney area loomed large, so I prepared for a huge leap of faith towards more independence. Armed with the knowledge that my employers were supportive of my move with them, it was "Canberra, here I come."

6

Flying The Nest

**Canberra Years
Bruce Hall, Residential College,
Australian National University**

I WAS FAREWELLED from Northbridge Uniting Church with a precious gift—a wooden plaque with the words "Be still, and know that I am God" (Ps. 46:10 NIV). Those beloved people knew how apt the present was for a woman who was on the verge of moving away from home for the first time. In the midst of my nervous excitement, the hanging reminded me to build my confidence in the God who created me. As I write this book, it is hanging in my study, continually alerting me to this important life lesson.

Winds of change blew our way. I felt strongly for my folks. In the space of months, I moved out, followed by my brother, who married and set up a home, leaving our parents empty-nesters virtually overnight.

If it were stressful for Mum and Dad for their offspring to fly the coop, then it was also a challenge for me. I moved into Bruce Hall, a residential college primarily for students attending the Australian National University in Canberra. However, the warden of the college was also expansive in his welcome of people living with physical disabilities. There were at least three other resident "wheelies" who formed part of the national capital's workforce.

For the next five years, a matchbox of a single student's room gradually morphed into my miniscule home. It was sparsely decorated with a brown carpet, small sink, and desk. Fortunately, the room was adjacent to a communal bathroom with a disability-designed shower. The communal dining room was a long trot downstairs on Canadian crutches, but I was blessed to have assistance with household chores from a Christian student on site.

Why am I recounting these minutiae of domestic arrangements? For young, strapping students, this was part of life, but for a tortoise-walking, crutch-carrying novice to independent existence, the new routine stretched every inch of my being. My heavy eyelids and drooping head signified frequent tiredness. My sleep was sometimes disturbed by the youthful exuberance of students, yelling in the corridors at night as they experimented with the "freedoms" of alcohol.

Canberra can be freezing in winter. Temperatures plummet to seven degrees below zero Celsius (19.4 degrees Fahrenheit) on occasion. Without shelter, my car was parked out in all weathers. While balancing on Canadian crutches, I used a credit card to scrape the thick morning frost off the car windows. Alternatively, a kind friend would throw a bucket of warm water on the car—a much less painstaking option. There was sometimes ice on the ground. In fear and trembling, I would literally skate on my crutches. In my fantasy, I was performing the ballet *Swan Lake*, but sometimes I fell in a most un-swan-like manner.

On a severe wintry occasion, I returned to my room after attending a conference. My bones were stiff and muscles tight with cold, my teeth chattering. I could hardly move. I turned on the heater, lights, electric jug, and electric blanket—actions which promptly blew the fuse and blacked out the rooms on the entire corridor. Mortification plus.

For all the negative aspects of university living in a cold climate, there were enormous positives as well. How can I forget the rich exposure to different people, disabilities, cultures, and religions? The residential college attracted many international visitors, including African, Thai, and Asian academics, with whom I was privileged to share table. Mealtime conversation was spiced with entrancing stories. The friendships I developed were priceless. Those years were marked with laughter, vibrancy, and my fascination with other cultures.

The beauty of the scenery and imaginative tourist attractions wove their magic around my heart. Autumn was heralded with bright red, yellow, and orange-flamed poplars. Spring with its abundant pink and white blossoms announced new hope and vitality after the icy barrenness of winter. The university campus was minutes away from the National Botanic Gardens, where I was a frequent weekend visitor.

At the time I was working there, Canberra was still developing its urban identity. Architecturally it was a beautiful city, and geographically not far from rural surrounds, to which I was inextricably drawn. The city still had the community feel of a large modern country town, albeit with sophisticated infrastructure and amenities to match its national capital status. Behind its elegant facade, I noticed that poverty and the uglier side of life were skilfully hidden. However, this carefully planned hub of living appealed to my artistic and cultural sensitivities, with a feast of galleries, theatres, museums, parks, gardens, and architecture to enjoy. Despite the occasional frigid extremes of climate, Canberra is still one of my favourite cities.

ACROD Film and Information Service, Canberra

I am forever grateful to ACROD for providing excellent opportunities in the national arena for me to network and learn the process of influencing political opinion. The largest proportion of my work in the Film and Information Service in the new, wheelchair-accessible building of ACROD involved cataloguing and answering copious research enquiries in the disability field through correspondence, phone, and face-to-face contact.

However, other opportunities also unfolded. I became a member of the National Library's Advisory Committee on Library Services for People with Disability. One of the big projects in this capacity was the compilation of a national directory of library and Information services for people with disability.

The International Year of Disabled Persons in 1981 proved to be a wonderfully expanding experience to be a part of. It succeeded in raising awareness about disability. For us, it was all noses to the grindstone, but what fun we had too. I was sometimes involved in publicity shots for posters. I remember posing in the lush grounds of Commonwealth Park in Canberra. As a Canadian crutch user, I "adopted" someone else's husband and child for a day to depict photographically a happy family playing in a green space. Perhaps I could have made a mint of money had I chosen a modelling career!

Travel by plane to other states in Australia was made possible for me as secretary to the National Committee on Epilepsy. Mounting displays at national conferences was also a great opportunity for me to meet and sit at the feet of disability experts while they delivered informative lectures.

Writing articles in disability magazines was another activity I grew to enjoy. I love playing with words, especially to raise awareness. Words can be humorous, playful, creative, and scholarly. Each type has their role in sneaking around a person's heart, mind, and spirit to possibly change his or her understanding of what it is to be human.

ACROD played host to overseas visitors, some of whom were fellowship scholars wishing to learn from the Australian scene. I was asked to share hospitality for a number of months with Ellen (fictitious name), a visiting American scholar and songwriter with a wide grin.

On one occasion, this high-spirited extrovert and I were walking down the streets of Canberra during the evening. As she danced on a Canadian crutch, she sang at the top of her contralto lungs the words of one of her folksy compositions, "It is hip to be crip." As a fairly reserved introvert, racing on my sticks to keep up with her, I felt like the whole world was glaring at us. All I wanted to do was sink quietly into oblivion down the nearest drain. But even in these memorable moments, I was touched by Ellen's friendliness and appreciation.

Canberra City Uniting Church

I linked up with the local Uniting Church in the city centre. The congregation attracted university students, public servants, and academics. It was a magnet for people from all over the world—Africans, Europeans, and Pacific Islanders, to name a few. This was the beginning of happy friendships, leadership opportunities, and Christian growth.

Hospitality was a wonderful gift of the gathering. I could not believe the genuine warmth of welcome when I was invited for a meal to a friendly couple's home. We were also blessed to have a jovial yet caring minister. A great preacher, he was also pastoral. His preaching emphasised the humanity of Jesus. I was captivated by a sermon on the heart-rending battle of Jesus to do the will of God in the garden of Gethsemane. Jesus seemed to be very real and grounded, not just a divine, remote figure.

Our minister was ably assisted by a dedicated, retired ministerial couple. They were wonderfully pastoral people who nurtured young adults by conducting Bible studies and opening their home for food and conversation.

Like all churches worth their salt, City Uniting encouraged the ministry of those attending. I found my niche in hospital visiting and organising seminars, as well as taking the occasional part in church services.

Theological College Recruitment Day

One day, I ventured into the deep and attended a seminar in Canberra. Its purpose was to inform participants of what was on offer at the Uniting Church's theological college—the training facility for Uniting Church ministers.

At this initial stage of enquiry, I was mildly interested in their curriculum. However, mild interest deepened into a mixture of yearning and unsettlement as the day progressed. What was the catalyst to this change of heart? Two young theological students were charged with leading a devotional segment that day. The Bible reading chosen related to the call of Moses to liberate the Israelites from slavery in Egypt.

> Now Moses was tending the flock of Jethro his father-in-law, the priest of Midian, and he led the flock to the far side of the wilderness and came to Horeb, the mountain of God. There the angel of the LORD appeared to him in flames of fire from within a bush. Moses saw that though the bush was on fire it did not burn up. So Moses thought, "I will go over and see this strange sight—why the bush does not burn up."

When the LORD saw that he had gone over to look, God called to him from within the bush, "Moses! Moses!" And Moses said, "Here I am."

"Do not come any closer," God said. "Take off your sandals, for the place where you are standing is holy ground." Then he said, "I am the God of your father, the God of Abraham, the God of Isaac and the God of Jacob." At this, Moses hid his face, because he was afraid to look at God.

The LORD said, "I have indeed seen the misery of my people in Egypt. I have heard them crying out because of their slave drivers, and I am concerned about their suffering. So I have come down to rescue them from the hand of the Egyptians and to bring them up out of that land into a good and spacious land, a land flowing with milk and honey … And now the cry of the Israelites has reached me, and I have seen the way the Egyptians are oppressing them. So now, go. I am sending you to Pharaoh to bring my people the Israelites out of Egypt."

But Moses said to God, "Who am I that I should go to Pharaoh and bring the Israelites out of Egypt?"

And God said, "I will be with you. And this will be the sign to you that it is I who have sent you: When you have brought the people out of Egypt, you will worship God on this mountain." (Exod. 3:1–12 NIV)

Moses proceeds to give God excuses as to why he cannot go through with the mission, his lack of eloquence being the main objection. However, God does not take no for an answer and provides Aaron, Moses's brother, as a companion.

Scripture can be powerful, if I am receptive enough to listen to its timeless messages. Moses was tending sheep when, unexpectedly, he sensed the glowing holiness of God in an unspectacular thorn bush. He appreciated the sacred moment in ordinary surroundings. Moses's divine nudge was not merely for encouragement of his spirit, but to help him discern the voice of God identifying the need of his oppressed people.

Unlike Moses, I was not about to ask a political favour of an Egyptian ruler. However, Moses's life and mine connected at the point of God's call to a new phase of life. Not only that, our common awareness of our seeming inadequacy for a monumental task struck a deep chord with me.

Like Moses, as I considered the possibility of studying for the ministry, I could think of all the excuses why it could never work. Like Moses, I felt I was not verbally eloquent. I wondered whether I was hiding behind the barrier of my disability to avoid more compassionate responsibility in a bigger arena. At that stage of my life I was also not aware of any wheelie ministers who had taken on the ministerial challenge. My knowledge was adequate enough to realise that, superficially at least, my small piece in the big jigsaw puzzle of ministry would not be a cosy fit.

If I did go ahead with theological study, it would mean uprooting from my favourite city, studying for three more years, and being somewhat of a trailblazer, in terms of becoming a minister with a moderate to severe disability. It all sounded daunting and yet exciting at the same time. Divine nudges can be disturbing and unsettling. They turn your life upside down.

Little by little, I sensed God's leading. Just as in the Moses story, in which God provided a companion in Aaron, I was convinced in my heart that help would be forthcoming in the event of obstacles. I was under no illusions that there would be many hurdles to successfully navigating the rigorous selection process. The Uniting Church is fond of saying, "A personal call to ministry is not enough. It must always be tested and discerned by the faith community."

So began the series of interviews to discern whether I had the gifts necessary for the exercise of ordained ministry. I found the interviewers to be open, welcoming, and yet understandably thorough in their comments and questioning. I did not expect, nor did I receive, any favours. Finally, after five stages of exploratory conversations, the final determination was positive. I was cleared for take-off, due to begin study in Sydney the following year.

In my travel towards ordained ministry, some people observed, "You are following in your father's footsteps." This assessment was incomplete. I believe God's call on a person's life is uniquely given, even though in my case, I was immersed from a young age in the strong value of ministerial service. The shape of my ministry, through different circumstances and gifting, turned out to be vastly different to my dad's.

In addition, Dad often said to Mal and me, "Don't go into the ministry unless you cannot possibly stay out of it." In other words, the lure of God's invitation must be stronger than any desire to be a carbon copy of anyone else.

7

Forging A Path To Ministry

Enfield Years
United Theological College, Enfield

THE SCHOLARLY PRINCIPAL, Rev. Dr Graeme Ferguson's welcome speech to the starry-eyed first-year students was as commanding as it was memorable. I paraphrase his message. While the recall is not verbatim, the essential message was crystal clear.

> You will cast your eyes around the room and wonder why so-and-so is studying for ministry. You are all so different. For the first year ever, the majority of you are women. You will reap the benefits of your strong-minded female student predecessors who have paved the way for you. We have overseas students from Japan and the Philippines. We have a person in wheelchair. Some of you are in your fifties. You will wonder, "How come?" Similarly, when the time comes as we enter the kingdom of heaven, I am sure

we will all be surprised… "the kingdom will be full of oddballs." God's love—God's call is inclusive.

He then asked me to explain to the class how my classmates could help me (or not) most appropriately. A very sensitive response!

Not only was support forthcoming, but the physical accessibility of the building was addressed as well. Two ramps—one at the front entrance and one to the chapel—were erected at the college to make movement easier for my wheelchair. Laughter and fun crackled in the air as I was designated to cut the red ribbon to officially "open" the new structures.

These actions, symbolising welcome and justice, were the fruit of the deep spirituality of the lecturers. An example of such faith was found in the principal's uplifting prayers for his students. After absorbing their pastoral power, I felt I could fly on eagle's wings.

I relished my freedom of theological exploration and did not feel confined by having to hold to a strong fundamentalist position of belief. I took like a moth to a flame to pastoral theology. The subject combined the skills of psychology and counselling with Christian spirituality and understanding of the place of God in an individual's or community's life.

How do I summarise three years of theological formation and education for ordained ministry in a few words? I found it a privilege to sit with experienced yet compassionate lecturers and students, young and old. We learned in-depth biblical studies, Christian theology, church history, social history of the church, social justice, Greek, spiritual formation, counselling, field education placements, worship, preaching, and more. The small class sizes encouraged a personal, pastoral approach to education. It was more difficult to hide the fact that I was not up to speed in reading and reflection. Ignorance or laziness could not blend into anonymity!

Grappling with important issues of life was an intellectual luxury. In addition to the blessing of learning, this grappling was demanding—not only academically, but also personally. We were challenged to gain self-insight. We were confronted with our blind spots and weakness. We were encouraged to work individually on assignments and in teams as well.

To use a cooking metaphor, we were pummelled like dough, rolled with a rolling pin, thinned like pastry, pronged with forks to let the air through, spiced, filled with fruit, and placed in a heated oven for maturing. This process aimed to develop qualities of sensitivity, reflection, and cultural understanding. We were encouraged to read widely and grow spiritually, to make us ready to begin ministry not just in churches but also in a range of community settings. The goal was not to mould us into a single cookie-cutter style of ministry where one size fits all, but to recognise the God-given diversity we possessed.

What were some important insights among the myriad that I gleaned in this time?

Evangelism: We will not argue people into the kingdom, only love them into the kingdom.

Christian Life: Hold on in the darkness to what you have learned in the light. Also, faith has an individual dimension in expression, but comes to fruition in the experience of community. Discerning the will of God is not just an individual exploration. Its richness needs to be confirmed in the life of the community.

Worship: In designing creative worship expressions, there is considerable freedom within the givens of the structure. When preaching, do not let your attire detract from the strength of your message. In other words, do not wear sparkling jewellery or jazzy clothes which will distract the congregation into a fashion critique. Simplicity is an appropriate choice to enable the strength of the Christian message to shine.

Church Leadership: In terms of introducing change to a church or community, we were encouraged not to change much for six months, in order to build trust with our congregation or community. It was vital to uncover first the history, values, and people dynamics.

Pastoral Care: The ability of a person to wade through personal crises will be improved if the quality of pastoral care given at the time of challenge is good.

Ministry: Rather than bringing God into the community, ministry is a about recognising the presence and activity of God, who is already alive and active.

Biblical Studies: I developed a love of the Hebrew Psalms, appreciating their richness and honesty for faith today.

Jesus Christ: The humanity of Jesus and his rich compassion for those who didn't quite fit attracted me. His ministry was inclusive rather than exclusive.

First-Year Field Education Placement

I was attracted to the opportunity of undergoing four hundred hours of clinical pastoral education at a major hospital in my first year at college. I was assigned to specific wards for visiting patients. I was not prepared, though, for the intensity of the interview process to ascertain whether I was a suitable applicant. After a couple of hours of in-depth questioning about my approach to life, motivation, weaknesses, and strengths, I felt as if I had been run over by a bus.

I gathered my shattered self together to receive the news that I had been accepted. There followed challenging weeks of visiting, and of preparing written records of patients' conversations for analysis in group and individual supervision. The aim of this process was to increase our self-awareness and pastoral sensitivity towards those recovering in hospital. I benefited greatly from the skilful leadership of our pastoral educators, and the opportunities to lead worship in the hospital chapel.

Second-Year Field Education Placement

While studying at the theological college nearby, with the agreement of Wesley Mission, I lived in a cottage adjacent to a mission-run residential facility called Pinaroo, dedicated to young folk with intellectual disability. The arrangement, recognised by the theological college as a portion of my field education requirements, was that I act as a pastoral presence for the residents and staff, in return for accommodation. I joined the residents for their evening meals in a communal dining room, engaging them in conversation. I occasionally conducted a Christian devotional message with them.

Accompanying residents to Sunday night church at the mission was one of my duties. At the time, the mission was under the pastoral leadership of Rev. Gordon Moyes, an evangelical minister with a confident, well-researched preaching style. I learned much about the art of preaching and the breadth of the social welfare arm of the mission. In fact, it was helpful preparation in my later vocation as a chaplain.

Some months later, after I had been away on holiday from Pinaroo, I returned to "my" cottage to find that four other residents with disabilities—three women and one man—had moved in without consultation with me. I had never lived with anyone outside family before, let alone a man. I admit to being rather miffed at the time, because I perceived this to be an intrusion on my personal and study space. One of the challenges of communal living was seeing a pretty blue top I owned and loved on the chubby proportions of another woman resident. "What is yours is mine, and what is mine is me own!"

This semi-independent living initiative, though, was meant to assist the residents to get used to more independence from institutional living. It was part of a bigger plan to transition some people from Pinaroo through this halfway house into their own group home. Despite my initial huffing and puffing, I realised that this would ultimately be beneficial for them. I discovered the difficult challenge that Mother Teresa, the tireless worker among the poor of Calcutta, had offered: "It is just accepting [God], as he comes into our life, accepting whatever he wants to take from us, making use of us as he wants, putting us where he wants without our being consulted."[1]

My flatmates and I took a while to get to know each other. We had days of laughing and times of clashing. On occasions, I played referee during disagreements. But a warm memory involves one of the residents, an accomplished cook. She sometimes prepared for us a beautiful roast lamb dinner. Such a gift lubricated the wheels of our community life.

The ministry with these people was not one-way, though. On one occasions, a light globe in the main hallway of Pinaroo had blown. A resident called out to me as I made my way back to my cottage for the evening. "Hang on a minute, Heather. I'll go and get a light globe so you don't fall down the stairs." His thoughtfulness from an unexpected place hit the spot at my genuine point of need. Walking down flights of stairs at the best of times was a scary challenge for me on Canadian crutches. The Bible verse that tempered my fear was "The eternal God is your refuge and underneath are the everlasting arms" (Deut. 33:27 NIV).

When I eventually left Pinaroo at the conclusion of three years of study, its residents and staff were sad to part with me, and I with them. I remember a male flatmate with black, spiky hair and thick-lensed glasses. He had little speech capacity. Unexpectedly, he vented his frustration at my leaving by pulling my hair and shaking my head. I was not particularly concerned, as this vigorous gesture was totally uncharacteristic. I interpreted it to mean that he did not want me to go, which was actually very touching. Fortunately there was a caring staff member nearby to help him debrief.

While Pinaroo was often a stretching time for me, especially while studying, the environment kept me grounded. I was helped in my reflections by the book *Road to Daybreak* by Henri Nouwen. Nouwen was a Catholic priest who was asked to be a pastor to people with intellectual disabilities and their helpers as they sought to live in Christian community together in Canada. His musings on his ministry affirmed the inestimable value of people, regardless of intellect. He also offered the insight that one of the gifts that people with varying levels of cognitive ability have is the potential to be our teachers, creating community and compassion around them.

More Second-Year Educational Experiences

Kings Cross and Visit to a Homeless Shelter

Kings Cross is a red-light district of Sydney, where the nightlife is flamboyant, pubs are full, homelessness is common, and ladies of the night wander the streets. Part of our training for ministry was to walk incognito at night in small groups into this area and to reflect on what we observed.

One image particularly sticks in my mind. A young man dressed in a black leather jacket, barely twenty years old, staggered noisily yet uncertainly from a pub. I wondered whether he would make it home, wherever home was. He promptly vomited vigorously on the pavement. I could not help thinking, "What a waste of a young person's potential!" I wondered whether there was anyone in his life who cared what happened to him. He cut a lonely figure.

We visited a homeless shelter. I was struck by the sheer number of people who wandered in and out for accommodation, a bit of tucker, welfare assistance, and a chat with a friendly face. The cramped conditions and the lack of privacy in the sleeping quarters were eye-openers. People slept in double bunks. Personally, this exposure pulled me up short at a time when my feathers were being ruffled. Here was I, living with a roof over my head at Pinaroo, complaining that I had to share a house with three or four residents with intellectual disability. Seeing the homeless shelter, I realised that my living conditions were palatial in comparison.

Floundering in the Valley

In my second year, I became severely depressed. The novelty of educational opportunity had worn off, and study was a hard slog. Theological education can be very intense. Apart from an essay load which made me feel like a sausage machine, churning out work at lightning pace, significant self-reflection was required. We were encouraged to write personal journals, examining our motivations and pondering the meaning of life and ministry.

With my disability, tenacious doubts gripped me like a vice. Would I ever be able to be a minister? The ministers I knew moved around with the speed of racehorses at the Melbourne Cup. The model of ministry I had observed relied on being physically agile. How could a tortoise like me ever survive?

There was no specific, external trigger event, but on one black day at college, I wandered around in an inky cloud that choked me. I could not envisage a future, even though I remembered my assignments to date had been successfully completed and I had received early affirmations. For those strangling hours, I seriously contemplated suicide. I even thought about how I would accomplish it. A handful of pills would end the misery and lack of hope I felt.

What stopped me? Perhaps it was the thought of the effect of my death on friends and family. There were no visible guardian angels or swift magical interventions to "kiss it better," though. In fact, the next day I was still beleaguered by the black dog. I do not remember any significant conversations which lifted the veil. Instead, one comment from a classmate struck me as strongly ironic and isolating. She said, "You look happy today." I place no blame on her for her ignorance; for that period, I was the mistress of disguise. To admit to such depressive darkness seemed incongruous in a woman studying for the Uniting Church ministry.

How does one resolve such a wretched divide within oneself? Plodding through the mire, moment by moment, was my short-term solution. Longer-term healing, though, lured me back to a more positive mental space where I could experience some wholeness. Again, reading life-giving books was a godsend—literally.

One such book was *The Wounded Healer* by Henri Nouwen, a pastoral care author whom I grew to appreciate greatly. The profound message I gleaned from this treasure was not to ignore or hide wounds. Rather than stuffing hurts up our jumpers so that no one can see them, we need to reflect on the impact they have on our lives, bring them into the healing light, and see how their presence can in fact lead to our sense of wholeness. Once we have bandaged and tended to our wounds, we can recognise their potential to create growth. We can then appropriately share our experience—not of perfection, but of hurt—and encourage another's journey toward healing.

Another book with a similar title was *J. B. Phillips: The Wounded Healer* by Vera Phillips and Edwin Robertson. This sensitive account tells the life of the New Testament scholar and initiator behind the Phillips paraphrase of the New Testament. The biography reveals what is little known about an internationally respected Christian man. He suffered severely from depression at times. What inspired me was that, because of his deep insights into the condition, he exercised a wonderful ministry of encouragement to fellow strugglers. It was not a ministry from a superior "holier than thou" level, but one offered as an equal. Our wounds, rather than being a source of shame, can be a source of hope. In a strange way, strength can be found in weakness. Such a book helped me to integrate my Christian faith and my humanity.

Another book struck a chord with me. I do not recall its title, but I was profoundly impressed by its message. The author declared that depression is not a state to be feared. The experience is similar to labour pains before birth. Depression has the potential to point to new insights and opportunities, if we are attentive to the meanings behind grieving and yearning.

In addition to these treasured literary gems, I was blessed to take a class called "Pastor as Person." The strong learning imprinted on my brain was that God calls us to ministry as the unique people we are, with the specific talents we have. We are not a copy of anyone else's ministry model. Our own style of ministry is shaped by the limitations, wounds, gifts, and potential inside each of us.

What a tremendous affirmation of God's cherishing of my own personhood. I realised that it was absolutely OK to be me. In fact, to be anyone else would not be faithful to the dream God has for me.

Third-Year Educational Experiences

Third-Year Field Education Placement

As part of my field education placement, I spent three-quarters of a day on one pastoral visit. A mum of an adult with an intellectual disability was willing to share her home with me. Much as I enjoyed her company, I felt guilty about the length of time I stayed. I was uneasy about the inefficiency of my time management with pastoral care.

My supervisor helped me to see that the widowed mum probably needed that extended time to talk about issues that were confronting her. He helped me to see that ministry is not just a list of tasks to be completed in a certain time, but rather living a Christ-like lifestyle, at whatever speed is necessary and possible.

Spiritual Direction

Our theological education emphasised the academic side of learning, but we were encouraged to spend time with a spiritual director to nurture our inner life with God. What a blessing a local Catholic teaching brother was to me. Many of our Catholic brothers and sisters have a deep understanding of the history of Christian spirituality, and possess an intimate connection with the divine One. For a person like me, who can at times be a driven perfectionist, the time with my "Spirit friend" was a gentle balm.

One of the symptoms he uncovered in me was what he termed "a hardening of the oughteries." The goals I set myself, physically, emotionally, and spiritually, were impossibly high. My life's energy was motivated by the word *ought* rather than a sense of gentle responsiveness.

While at college, I was also introduced to the beauty of contemplative retreats. I reflected upon Scripture not just as an academic exercise, but as an instrument of personal and corporate transformation. I relished times of silence, both as an individual and in groups. These times were opportunities for me to receive God's gracious blessing, rather than always striving for more understanding, or more personal perfection. For me they were experiences of basking in the presence of a gentle Shepherd. These gatherings provided a springboard in later years for me to lead retreats for ministers.

Easter Journey

In 1985, my last year of theological training, I sat in the college chapel, waiting for our Easter celebration of the resurrection of Christ to begin. I looked down at the floor to see the large wooden cross which had lain there throughout Holy Week. To me, it was a powerful and precious reminder again of Jesus's suffering and of his being part and parcel of all human turmoil. More specifically, it reminded me of my suffering as a person with a disability. He knew what it was like to suffer hurt and to grieve. I felt that the crucifixion was a symbol that he enters into and shares my suffering in an intimate way. Also, as the apostle Paul writes in Romans 8:17, if I was a co-heir with Christ, I somehow shared in his suffering as well. The idea gave me strength to cope with the struggle of being disabled.

That was not the end of the story, though.

As the chapel service began, two people came in, took up the cross, and joyfully shouted, "He is risen. He is risen." I did not see the cross again.

The feeling of abandonment slugged me like a gunshot. The suffering Christ had left me behind. He was entering into a joyful triumph, which I certainly did not feel at that stage.

I am sure good people never daydream in church, but that day, at that moment, I did. I saw a clear picture of myself running through a beautiful field, graceful and free, unrestricted by tight muscles.

Abruptly the reverie stopped. I looked down. I was not in the field. I was still imprisoned in my wheelchair. I froze.

The rest of the service was a blur until it came to Communion. A piece of bread was handed to me. I heard the words, "This is my body, broken for you." My angry thoughts spat their venom in my own private challenge to Christ. "You think you're the only one with a broken body—what about mine? You have no monopoly on suffering. How dare you leave me behind!"

I was shaking for the rest of the day. I sobbed that night, shocked at the strength of my feeling and deeply hurt by the sense of betrayal. It was not a happy Easter.

A couple of months later, my fellow students were studying the gospel of John in class, specifically the resurrection appearance of Christ to the disciples through the locked door. We focused on John 20:25. This verse contains the words of the disciple Thomas. "Unless I see the holes that the nails made in his hand and can put my finger into the holes they made and unless I can put my hand into his side, I refuse to believe." Then, in verse 27, comes Christ's gracious invitation: "Put your finger here; see my hands. Reach out your hand and put it in my side." (NIV)

Why was the writer of John so particular in these points? Sure, he wanted to make clear to his readers that the earthly Jesus and the resurrected Christ were one and the same person, and that there was no deception.

However, to me there was one more vital point which our lecturer explained. (Bless her!) Christ's wounds were not forgotten in the resurrection. They were not blotted from his memory or blithely swept aside into insignificance. To Christ, his suffering was still an important part of his resurrected identity.

In addition, his wounds, the assault on his body, were used in a dramatic way to reassure Thomas in his wavering faith. They were a pin pointer to a changed relationship for Thomas.

These words were like a healing ointment to my hurting soul. Crazy underlines and a cluster of excited exclamation marks danced on my lecture notes. It was as if I was afraid that I would forget such a beautiful insight. I felt like jumping up and down on the classroom tables, I was so happy. However, such things are not done in theological colleges!

The resurrected Christ remembers his suffering and uses it to fan the flame of flickering faith. If we are partners with Christ, he remembers our struggles and encourages another who is a questing Thomas.

Ordination

The end of my third year of study saw the successful completion of my ministerial course—a time of celebration, having accomplished, by the generous grace of God, a hard-won goal.

Before I could be ordained—that is, commissioned in a special church service by the Uniting Church—we had to ensure that my first ministerial posting was in place. Earlier in the year, I had been asked to write a paper on the specific issues which needed to be considered in paving the way for a placement for me as a person with a disability. This I completed with great energy, expressing a strong wish for a chaplaincy ministry rather than a congregational placement.

Later, I was alerted to an advertisement for a chaplain to minister to people with intellectual disabilities. The position was interstate, a long way from home. After much soul searching, I applied, recognising that my experience at Pinaroo would be helpful in supporting my application. I recall personally posting the application in a heavy downpour, juggling the package on my Canadian crutches. As I heard the sound of the letter plonk into the red post box, tears streamed down my face, mingling with drops of rain. The cost of ministry for this family-minded adventurer would be great, but I also knew that the providential God would be walking into the future with me.

With news of my successful Queensland appointment, planning for my ordination service in my Canberra congregation could begin. Here was another step towards spiritual maturity. The church building, my beloved spiritual home, was to be demolished the week before the service, making way for a new sacred space. I was devastated. These bricks and mortar symbolised for me the love and nurturing of the congregation. My old attachments had to be painfully dismantled to make way for new connections. I was learning the lesson that my faith was always on the move, not confined to a specific building. I was to be part of a pilgrim people, always on the way.

The ordination service was conducted in a builders' hut on the site of the vanished church. My fears of celebrating in a dark grey building amid debris and discarded tools were allayed. Faithful church women decorated the interim dwelling, leaving it festooned with colourful flowers. An inspiring service was conducted in the presence of friends, family, and the church community. The ordination was sealed with the laying on of hands, symbolising the presence of the Holy Spirit. It was a wonderful affirmation which crowned hard years of study and reflection. Joyful faith could not be suppressed, nor could the presence of a vibrant God be confined to one prized building.

A gift I cherished was a red stole, presented as part of my liturgical dress. The colour represents the presence of the Holy Spirit. A dear friend had exquisitely embroidered it in silver and gold thread. The symbols chosen had great significance for me personally: the cross (Jesus's identification with suffering humanity) and a gold crown (a celebration of Christ's eventual victory over the forces that crush and demean us).

The day before the service, I was interviewed by a journalist with the *Canberra Times* newspaper. The trip to the interview was an experience. Severely visually impaired himself, the reporter was nonetheless capable of helping wheel me from the car at the appointed time. The teamwork began when I beeped my horn so he could locate where my car was parked. He lifted my manual wheelchair from the boot. After we crossed the road, he tipped the wheelchair (with me in it) on its back wheels and lifted me up about six steps, which I had counted beforehand. Yes, I admit to breathing a silent sigh of relief when we both made it to the venue safely.

I was later to reflect on the nature of mutual ministry in this unusual scenario. The reporter and I used our differing abilities to compensate for our physical limitations. I was his eyes; he was my muscle.

Another gift he left me was from a surprising quarter. An account of my ordination service made the front page in the capital's newspaper the next day, complete with a jubilant photo of the new minister.

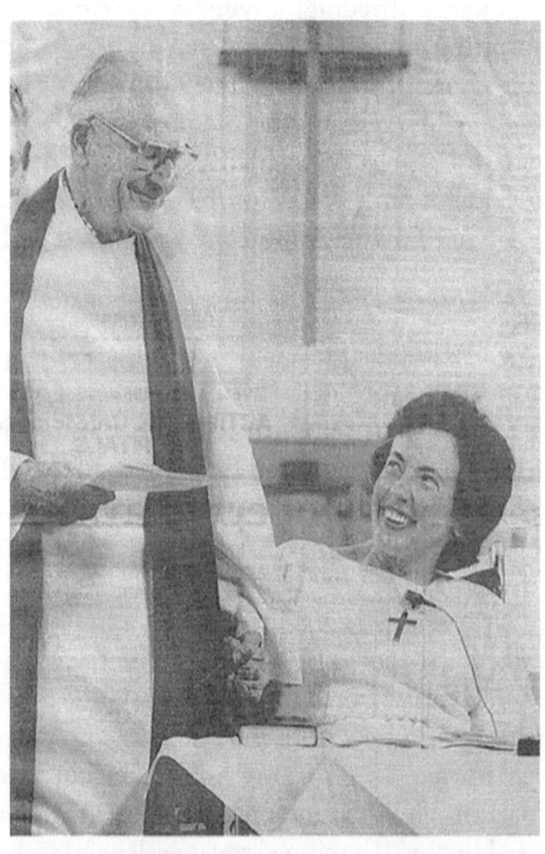

Credit: *Canberra Times* 17 February 1986 (by permission)
Photographer: Martin Jones/Fairfax Syndication

8

Adventure in the Subtropics

First Ministry Placement

A WHIRLWIND OF activity accompanied my move to Queensland, sixteen hours' drive north from Sydney. My new home in the working-class city of Ipswich was sunny and airy. The nearby Air Force base made its noisy presence felt, with huge jets thundering through the sky.

How would I describe the city itself? It enjoyed only basic amenities. But what Ipswich lacked in inspiring town planning, it made up for in beautiful rural surroundings of rich agricultural land. In summer, the humid heat was energy-sapping, reaching thirty to forty degrees Celsius (86 to 104 degrees Fahrenheit). On those days, my motivation to change the world in three days was sadly depleted. At the other extreme, I remember valiantly preaching a sermon through chattering teeth in a cavernously cold church when the winter temperature plummeted to four degrees below zero. Ipswichites were bred tough!

Climate was not the only challenge. There were residents, including railway workers, on low incomes. I met many who scrimped and scraped to make ends meet. Financial hardship and life in very basic housing was common. Exposure to this side of life was sobering for this middle-class girl.

I was fascinated that some words were used differently from state to state. What I knew in New South Wales as a *street directory* was now a *refidex*. What I called a *dressing table* was a *duchess* in Queensland. What I termed *frankfurts*, red fingers of processed meat, were now *cheerios*. Friendly rivalry often became apparent between the Queensland "banana-benders" and the New South Wales "Mexicans," south of the border.

In those early days, my wry sense of humour alerted me to similarities between my new situation and the biblical experience of the Jews captive in Babylon. I asked the same question voiced by the exiled Jews who yearned for home: "How can we sing the songs of the Lord while in a foreign land?" (Ps. 137:4 NIV) The feeling of strangeness melted slowly as my community gradually grew around me. Cleaning, shopping, gardening, meal preparation and neighbourly support were graciously provided. Old friends lived within a reasonable distance, and their offers to whisk me away on country picnics were appreciated.

The diverse ministerial team members and their families, with whom I worked, were also welcoming. Who were they? A capable, entrepreneurial superintendent provided the vision and direction for the wide-ranging mission. An academically-minded minister with a huge pastoral heart was a major part of the team. The energetic children's worker delighted in running camps and other activities. The warm-hearted aged care chaplain with a quirky sense of humour was a wonderful team member too. A forward thinker worked with young adults, and a cheery Sri Lankan was a skilled parish minister. We were all ably assisted by managerial, administrative, and welfare staff and flanked with numerous volunteers.

This large Uniting Church mission was community-oriented. Included in its outreach was a base for Lifeline, a reputable phone and face-to-face counselling service. As well as a number of aged care facilities in the area, there were several worshipping congregations.

Chaplaincy Ministry

The main focus for my work was with people with intellectual disability and their families. The existing strength of the mission in this sector was largely due to the passion and vision of the mission superintendent and his capable wife. I discovered that their adult daughter had an intellectual disability. Their strong push for the establishment of these important services originated from a desire for a good, well-rounded quality of life for their daughter and many others like her. In my years of experience since, I have learned that the impetus for innovative services often originates from a strong personal story and an expressed sense of need. I admire such folk for persistence in seeing a dream fully realised.

Part of this outreach included two facilities for supported employment for people with cognitive difficulties. Together, they existed under the banner of Light Industries. Goods were assembled and packaged in one building for local suppliers. A laundry on another site operated to service local health and accommodation providers. The repetitive tasks required in both these services are often well suited to the skills of employees with special needs.

My role included visiting and supporting employees and staff as part of a bigger welfare team. I conducted regular devotional services at both facilities. I learned quickly that speaking simple words, with frequent use of pictures and concrete images, was most helpful to this particular audience. Conveying the Christian message with long-winded, abstract explanations was one sure way to elicit yawning and glazing over of the eyes.

With this in mind, I celebrated the coming of Christ with the lighting of Advent candles. Surely, this was a worshipful expression of the light of Jesus. However, one staff member chastised me privately, saying that the lighting of candles was pro-Catholic.

Some days later, I received an anonymous, strongly worded, anti-Catholic brochure through the mail, which disturbed me. Some of my best friends were Catholic, luminous examples to me of contemplative faith. The lighting of candles is a common expression of faith among Jews, Catholics, and Protestants. I found it hard to come to terms with such a lack of understanding.

Weddings

It was in the supported employment environment of Light Industries that I met young couples with intellectual disabilities. One duo asked me to marry them—an exciting time for them and a learning time for me as a first-time certified marriage celebrant. One of my lecturers at theological college warned his fledging ministerial students that when we conducted weddings, we should expect the unexpected. That advice certainly proved to be correct.

Friends, family, and colleagues gathered in one of our churches to celebrate the wedding. The groom was half an hour late, leaving his white-gowned bride anxiously circling the block in the wedding car. The service finally started, but the groom had forgotten the ring. Hastily, a work colleague loaned him his wedding band. As if that weren't enough, a loud thud interrupted my dulcetly intoned words of the marriage service. One of the bridesmaids had not eaten breakfast and fainted to the floor. Later, at the bride's home reception, dessert was served first to allow time for the main course to be cooked on a spit.

Despite these hiccups, the delightful couple were duly married in the presence of supportive friends—a triumph of love and teamwork.

The apprentice chaplain breathed a huge sigh of relief when the day of her first wedding was over.

A second, less formal wedding I was happy to conduct in my lounge room. The bridal couple were again employees of Light Industries. Two witnesses and a couple of friends supported them. Money was tight, so all the participants settled for casual attire: T-shirts and jeans.

A few minutes yet from the close of the quiet, informal ceremony, I was surprised by a request from the bride's matron of honour, who was cuddling her baby. She wondered, "Heather, can I please change my baby's nappy?"

Taken aback, I recovered and quietly said, "It won't be long now. We are nearly finished. We need to wait."

I chortled to myself, thinking that my former college liturgy lecturer, who put great stock in ordered precision in the design of worship, would have had apoplexy. Social niceties are part of an ongoing educational process for people with intellectual disabilities.

Again, the couple were married simply in the presence of people who loved them. Big finances and stiff formality were not necessary for a happy occasion to be celebrated.

How fondly do I remember being asked to conduct a "Reaffirmation of Marriage Vows" service! Young love is a delight to honour, but to witness the flourishing and stability of mature love is encouraging.

Learning on the Job

I led religious education classes in two schools catering for primary-grade children with special needs. In one class, I was grateful for the generous assistance of a Christian special education teacher, who happened to be the spouse of one of our ministerial team. Her skill in class discipline and her creative work on the blackboard were boosts to the spirit of one novice Scripture teacher. I had never in my life taught in a classroom, let alone one catering for special needs. Her easy communication and sense of humour made my tough job easier.

I occasionally visited a large residential facility for people with intellectual disabilities, during a transition period between institutional accommodation and small-group housing. My knowledge of the wider community welfare network expanded when I joined an inter-agency community group, aiming for co-ordination of services to people with intellectual disabilities.

I also became part of the planning teams for two recreational groups for people with learning difficulties. Crossroads, a Christian-based group with a strong recreational and educational thrust, was a thriving gathering for teens and young adults. We hosted guest speakers, enjoyed outings such as ferry trips, played games and sports, danced, and conducted devotions. "Pathfinders" was the name of an equivalent group for younger children.

Part of my emerging role was to raise awareness of disability among the churches. I was even asked to speak to a conference of disability service providers on the issue of educational experiences of young adults with disabilities. I thought this was a great honour, but it was also a learning curve for me.

I worked in tandem with a hand-signing interpreter for my presentation. I learned to appreciate the great skill of signers, who were often artistic in the use of specific hand gestures. The word for *bride*, for example, is formed with one clenched fist on top on another clenched fist, describing the one walking down the aisle carrying a bouquet. I also learned the importance of speaking at a slower speed, with reasonable gaps between sentences to allow the hand-signers to catch up. On other occasions, I noted signers were placed in a roster for large events such as conferences, so each could give their expressive hands a rest.

Another highlight was an invitation to lead a Synod Bible study. This state wide church forum consisted of church leaders around Queensland, who gathered annually to discuss policy matters, determine direction for the future, and be nourished in biblical reflection. I was required to speak in front of about two hundred members for about half an hour on a favourite Bible reading. I chose the gospel of John, chapter 20, and began my musings with the Easter experience I encountered in my last year of theological college. (See the section "Easter Journey" in Chapter 7.)

Needless to say, while it was an honour to be asked, it was also a daunting challenge for a thirty-something new minister to inspire the more experienced fathers and mothers of the state church who were sitting expectantly in front of me. My palms sweated profusely, and my breathing became shallow. However, God undertook for me, and I was staggered to receive a standing ovation at the end. Talk about relief!

Like other ministers on my team, I shared in the conduct of church services. Some Sundays the words flowed easily, while on others, preparation could be likened to squeezing water from a dry rag. The high personal expectations of preaching and the self-imposed pressure to perform well affected my creative juices. I lived the truth of the words, "In striving to be perfect, we mar what is well."6 However, I enjoyed sharing the gospel in intimate worship groups in our aged care facilities. This preference was a foreshadowing of the shape of my future ministry.

Pastoral work was my first love. In that capacity, I enjoyed visiting a softly spoken, yet spirited lady in her mid-fifties with severe rheumatoid arthritis. She was an intelligent wheelchair user in one of our aged care facilities. On bad-pain days, she was often bedridden. I was struck by her sense of humour, which seemed to soak through her severe discomfort. I wondered at the time, "Who is ministering to whom?" Perhaps the ministry was mutual. My regular contact with her heightened my awareness of the challenges of younger people whose high support needs force them to live with people much older than themselves. Elderly people share the same humanity, of course, but their interests and intellectual capacity are sometimes vastly different.

Another form of ministry emerged when I organised an arts and crafts event for the community. It was not a regular display of work, but rather a celebration of items which would be particularly enjoyed by people with visual impairments. There were artistic pieces crafted with different textures, rough and smooth, which could be felt with sensitive fingers. There were other items made with the wafting of fragrances to highlight the gift of smell. Other creations optimised the use of sound, such as bells and whistles. The overarching aim of the displays was to heighten our awareness of the senses through which our bodies engage with the world.

Recreation

My life outside of work was sometimes eventful. One day, after picking up my car from its regular service, I was shocked when the left front wheel suddenly fell off and rolled down the hill, as I continued to drive slowly on three remaining wheels. It pays not to think too much about the consequences had the oncoming car not deftly avoided the runaway object. I stopped as safely as I could, slowing my pounding heart.

On another occasion, I was fortunate to attend regular physiotherapy at the local hospital, to keep myself in trim. There I met a fellow patient, a man in his late twenties with dark curly hair. He was a double amputee and had only one arm. What disability! What struck me was his sheer determination to live life as normally as he could. His conversational style was easy, his attitude positive, and his biceps muscles on his remaining arm positively rippling! At the time of the encounter, I vowed that I would never complain again. Of course, I did grumble occasionally at my lot, but for that moment he was my hero and positive role model.

The year 1988 was Australia's bicentenary of western settlement. Brisbane, Queensland, played host to a massive international expo to mark this milestone. A number of nations were invited to mount expansive displays showcasing their national character, scenery, and cultural heritage.

Sir Llew Edwards, the overall director of this massive project, was a devoted Christian and a member of one of our Ipswich congregations. A humble man of great ability, he gathered multiple threads of capacity and skill to bring to life this wonderful dream. On my days off, I was fortunate enough to attend the expo on a number of occasions. As a person with a disability, I was particularly impressed with the detailed planning that was evident in the creation of an accessible transport network and disability-friendly exhibits. Such feats of thoughtfulness and ingenuity are possible after all!

Overall View

How do I sum up the significance of my ministry in Ipswich? As a green apprentice minister, I was indebted to capable mentoring from many. It is true that despite the support offered, I suffered bouts of homesickness, missing significant milestones in family life. However, my awareness of the effectiveness of community outreach in the Queensland church grew enormously. The church, if it remains isolated from genuine need, dies quickly. The central mission was a shining example of grounded, visionary and dedicated service. The compassionate people with whom I bonded for this time were indeed God's gift, both to me and to the Ipswich community.

9

Faithfulness Tested

Second Ministry Placement

WANTING TO MOVE to Sydney, closer to family, I sought an appointment as associate librarian at Camden Theological Library. I believe God had his hand in providing suitable accommodation. I stumbled on a quotation from an unknown source which fits the bill in this instance. "Coincidence happens when God chooses to remain anonymous." My dad happened to be researching in the library where I was to work. He started up a conversation with the then-superintendent of Parramatta Mission, who was also reading there. Two of his parishioners were looking for a tenant. I rented their wonderful one-bedroom flat in the wealthy, leafy neighbourhood of Castle Hill. My pharmacist landlords, with their extended family and black cat named Willie, were caring, neighbourly Christians. They proved to be a generous blessing.

The contrast between the blue-collar community of Ipswich, many of whose inhabitants were in Struggle Street, and the affluence now surrounding me could only be described as stark. I must admit to initially feeling uncomfortable. Some residents in this suburb had little exposure to the challenges of poverty.

The research centre which was to be my workplace for the next few years resourced the major education enterprise of the Uniting Church in New South Wales for both lay and ordained ministry. Housed in a beautiful new building surrounded by towering gums, the library was a gathering place for many as they sought to master the study of theology and its application to personal, social, and public life. Our collection consisted of journals, books, articles, and databases on subjects including biblical studies, church history, pastoral theology, worship, Christianity and culture, spirituality, multi-faith dialogue, and mission.

Together with the intelligent head librarian who was a walking encyclopaedia, a sociable library technician, and dedicated volunteers, we supported the educational needs of the many students and lecturers who passed through our doors. I thought that this new vocation would be a useful combination of librarianship skill and my theological training. My initial hopes were that I would spend a large proportion of time handling reference queries, with considerable people contact. But as time progressed, the needs of the library determined that I spend more time in the cataloguing area.

Other Ministries

While cataloguing theological books, I had opportunity for other ministries at this centre of learning. Once I was approached to fill in for a theological lecturer who had another engagement. He asked me to present a paper based on an essay I had written while a theological student. "Martin Luther's (Church Reformer) View of Marriage and Family Life" certainly did not slay the audience of twenty or so mature students, but the experience stretched me and hopefully added insight for ministers in formation.

Presenting only one lecture caused the sweat to form on my brow. Imagine the pressure on lecturers to produce high-quality information and challenging argument day in and day out.

I occasionally led worship in the college chapel, where students, staff, and lecturers gathered to sing, contemplate, and speak their devotion to God. A humorous aside to this custom related to my liturgical dress. College culture required that ministerial attire for worship leaders was formal. I wore a cream dress and a gold cross. The stoles around my neck were long and slim-line cloth, embroidered as liturgical bookmarks. Surely these were a fitting symbol of my double life as both librarian and minister!

Welcome respite from the robot-like cataloguing software programme was provided by my contact with ministerial students and lecturers. I renewed my appreciation for the dedication of overseas students. Learning English as a second language is hard enough without the added burden of understanding the highly abstract concepts of theology in English. Over time, our library collection catered more adequately to this specialised need. Tongan and Korean language material became more visible to meet the needs of a growing, multicultural Uniting Church.

I became a member of the Uniting Church Committee on Disability Awareness. Our thrust was to produce educational materials for Uniting Church congregations, to assist them in their ministry with people who live life a little differently. The small but passionate group, some of whom had lived experience of different kinds of impairments, produced pamphlets and a video as helpful resources for our state wide church.

What a memorable opportunity was afforded me during this ministerial placement when I attended the World Council of Churches Assembly in Canberra in 1991. Here was an international coming together of church leaders from different Christian denominations, including Greek Orthodox, African, and Korean Christians.

Spine-tingling worship according to different traditions was conducted each morning in a massive tent. I was totally mesmerised by the transcendent mystery of Greek Orthodox chanting. We were transported to the "heavenlies." In contrasting mood, spontaneous joy bubbled through the expressive body movements and brightly coloured costumes of the South Africans as they sang in exquisite harmony, giving glory to God.

The topic of disability provided a reflective theme for worship in this huge forum. In this context, I was asked to lead a prayer in front of hundreds of international visitors. To manage my nervousness, I had to remind myself that God alone was my audience. However, I was moved by the groundswell of support as I prepared for this awesome responsibility.

On another occasion at the Assembly, I was privileged to lead an elective on my personal experiences of the healing ministry. One of the big take-home messages from this international convention was that in our immense diversity of faith expression, I sensed a palpable unity among us.

Towards the end of my time at the library, I was honoured to form part of the team to support the new president-elect of the National Assembly of the Uniting Church in Australia. There was a moving church service to install her into her three-year term as a national church leader. During this worship experience, a few others and I laid hands on her, praying that she would be aware of the gift of the Holy Spirit of God, supporting her in this vital servant role.

On another occasion, I was asked to take part in the installation church service of the state moderator of New South Wales at the time. Both occasions were uplifting experiences for me.

Castle Hill Uniting Church and the Ministry of Crossroads

I worked at the library during the week and linked up with the Uniting Church congregation in Castle Hill on the weekends. There, I conducted an occasional church service and became an elder with pastoral responsibility.

After returning from a holiday with a Christian organisation which specialised in ministry to people with disability, I was inspired to establish a new venture. I saw the need for a local recreational group attracting adults with intellectual disabilities, based on a model with which I had been familiar in Ipswich. I invited the movers and shakers of Crossroads Queensland to guide us through the necessary steps to bring the vision alive.

Beginning this new project, I felt like bursting into a croaky rendition of the song "The Impossible Dream," from *West Side Story*. In my heart, though, I held on to the possibility that from tiny acorns, big oak trees grow. The ground swell of support from the church community gathered momentum as we inched our way forward. Enthusiasm was contagious.

We enlisted the help of a dedicated team of volunteers to run a monthly series of social, educational, recreational, and spiritual activities. Guest speakers on first aid, life skills, and hobbies added spice to our programme, which was geared towards about fifty participants. These were clients of special schools and group homes in the surrounding district. Family members who wished to come along were also welcome.

Intrepid volunteer photographers snapped their cameras at our Crossroads evenings, which added to the fun, bringing significance to each individual captured through the lens. We discovered this was a place where friendships were cemented and living skills were developed.

This energetic group lasted seventeen years, long after I left—a tribute to the creativity of the planning committee and the star power of volunteers. A satellite group of Crossroads was also begun at Castle Hill's sister church, Kentgrove Uniting Church.

A Movie and Its Aftermath

I like movies. Little did I realise the impact a movie called *My Left Foot* was to have on my equilibrium. It was a brilliantly acted, gutsy film about a young Irish man with cerebral palsy, who was raised in poverty. The focus on the sheer determination of both his mother and himself was palpable. The patient hero, with suppressed energy raging inside him, galvanised the strength of his left foot to propel his severely disabled body around, even up a flight of stairs in his home. In time, he discovered a penchant for writing, moving his foot to painstakingly tap the keys on his typewriter.

A normal story of triumph over incredible odds, you might say, but its profound effect on my body and emotions alerted me to yet another hidden story that needed to be unfurled and honoured within me.

During one scene of the movie, the main character is shown locked in his bedroom, brooding for many days in silent depression, much to the chagrin of his mother. She is at her wits' end to know what to do.

I identified strongly. My heart grasped the utter despair which exuded from the screen. My gut was churning, and I could not engage with my movie companion beyond civil, monosyllabic responses.

The following Monday, I filled in the day at work. My body, in robot mode, was present, but my mind was a thousand miles away. A mate, who was a counsellor working in an adjacent section, happened to come by (a divine nudge, perhaps?). He innocently asked, "How was your weekend?"

Little by little, the story tumbled out about the movie and my over-the-top, albeit internalised volcanic eruption. He listened skilfully, gently prodding, until my tears flowed. The character's angst mirrored my own frustrations with my imprisoned, "disabled" life in a way which scared the pants off me.

After my venting, he asked, "What now? What are you going to do now with these insights? How can you channel such strength constructively?" I was struck by the power of these questions.

Together, we hatched a plan for me to arrange a seminar on disability and the church, using my passion, interest, and contacts. Its aim was to encourage a more sensitive and welcoming Christian community for people who have disabilities. The event gathered together guest speakers and other interested participants from different Christian denominations to cross-fertilise ideas and energies.

For me personally, the planning ignited a fire of renewed purpose. The seminar's eventual success was a wonderful affirmation. Enhancing ministry with people experiencing disability, whether physical or intellectual, emerged as a recurring theme in my ministry.

Photographer: Ian Richardson

My biggest learning from this period was that grief over losses is nothing of which to be ashamed. If it is carefully nurtured with kindness, it will not be wasted, and will eventually be sublimated into positive action. Rather than being stuck as victims in sadness, there is great potential for lost ones who have good soul-friends to become energetic change-agents. Thank God for compassionately skilled companions armed with big handkerchiefs!

Hospital as a Patient

During my Castle Hill days, I was advised to have two separate surgical operations simultaneously. After surgery, I felt gutted—like twelve stretched guitar strings about to break. Apparently, I looked like a white corpse on a trolley as I was returning from the recovery room. I heard my parents' reassuring voices during the process of regaining consciousness, but I could not vocally respond. I held their hands and squeezed them to let them know I could hear them.

In the midst of intense physical restlessness, I heard the tender voice of an attending nurse calling to me out of oblivion, "You are doing very well." Those words were encouraging as I endured the pain of my strangled nerve endings.

My hospital bed was situated opposite an elderly woman patient who was a strongly professing Jehovah's Witness. I did not know her medical condition, but I do remember discussions her doctors had with her about the necessity for surgery for her life-threatening illness. As I understand it, Witnesses do not believe in blood transfusions. The medical professionals, in their argument for the vital importance of surgery, mentioned plasma transfusion.

She refused surgery. She eventually returned home—I believe, to die.

The memory of her distraught husband, a fellow Jehovah's Witness, carved itself deeply in my psyche. He was torn between the love of his wife, whom he wanted to cling to in this life, and their mutual, tenacious belief that blood transfusions were forbidden. His pained eyes and pleading voice spoke eloquently of his deep, anguished conflict.

In my own fragile post-operative state, I found this situation difficult to process. I make no judgement about the rightness or wrongness of the belief. I simply say that my heart wanted to reach out to him in compassion for the ethical and human dilemma in which he found himself.

If that were not enough to test my emotional resilience while in hospital, I was informed that one of our parishioners at church, an air force pilot on an F-111, was killed in a plane crash, leaving a young wife and two beautiful kids. In my lowered physical and emotional state, I remember announcing to those would listen, "Life is so very unfair!" I was not on the best speaking terms at that moment with God. Just as well that God was and is strong enough to cope with my anger.

Hospital as a Volunteer Chaplain

After recovery, I returned to work, but after five years at the library, it had become obvious that I was champing at the bit for a new phase of ministry. I yearned for more people contact and less computerised cataloguing in a back room. There was a limit to how engaging a conversation could be with a computer that was always prompting me to provide author, title, publisher, date, and classification number details. On occasions, the machine had the temerity to type back to me, "I think you have made an error." Was librarianship really the avenue to express my calling?

Having negotiated with my employers, I worked part-time at the library and the remaining time as a pastoral care volunteer at a local major hospital. This appeared to be a great idea to test the waters. The new area of voluntary work was like a breath of fresh air blowing through the curtains of my life. Having recently been hospitalised myself, I had a revitalised understanding of the experience of being a patient. Under the guidance of the senior chaplain, I visited many ill people—an experience which gave me fulfilment.

Unknown to him, one patient became my teacher. He was a young Middle Eastern immigrant. Our first conversation, I felt, was very positive. He seemed willing to share of himself deeply, and I committed to listening to his story carefully and compassionately. We parted on good terms.

My second encounter with him a few days later was quite different. He was reserved, monosyllabic in his responses, and ill at ease. Reading the signals, I discovered that this conversation was going to be short-lived. With the help of my supervisor, I gradually realised that sometimes people become embarrassed and feel exposed if they have shared at great depth too fast, too soon. In this patient's culture, confiding in a woman might not have been usual. I am grateful to him for the lesson he unwittingly taught me.

I threw my hat in the ring to be considered when the possibility emerged of a paid position as a Uniting Church chaplain at this hospital. However, the transition from volunteer to a paid position was not plain sailing. Some of the paid pastoral team had doubts about my capacity to cope physically with the work involved. One solution to the dilemma was to institute a trial period to determine whether their fears were justified. A mentor was appointed to assist me in discernment. I hired a motorised wheelchair to navigate the maze of corridors.

The trial period was helpful in pointing out challenges. To make a long story short, I decided to withdraw from the permanent position. The on-call work of pastoral emergency required that I stay some nights at the hospital. For this tortoise in a wheelchair to heave up from bed in the middle of the night, much less attend afterward to families in gut-wrenching crisis, seemed a mountain too high. My supervisor reflected that I need not appear on the scene at the speed of a knight on a white charger. Nevertheless, I felt that the wisdom required in being with people in emergency situations, such as death through drug overdose, had not yet ripened in my life. With a strange mixture of intense disappointment and relief that the pressure to make this work was finally over, I sensed this particular door of ministry was closing.

Waiting

If hospital chaplaincy was not possible, what then? The question haunted me with a ghost-like quality. I will never forget the kindness of a mental health chaplain who showed me around a psychiatric facility to discern whether this was a field of possible ministry for me.

While pastoral care in this setting is vital, I did not feel it was a good fit for me.

I wondered what God was up to. There were more closed doors than open ones. I had applied for a number of jobs, both in the so-called secular field and in the religious domain, without success. A friend reminded me that sometimes we need to wait for God to do his stuff, but waiting is never my strong point. In my myopic vision, God seemed to work exceedingly slow.

Finally, the principal of the theological college informed me of a promising development. He had received a phone call from an aged care facility on the South Coast of New South Wales. The manager wondered whether there was a theological student who would complete a field education placement for six months while they searched for a chaplain. The principal, who had been one of my lecturers, replied, "No, but I do happen to know of a lady who might fit the bill." God bless the principal!

I looked forward to meeting the staff at the retirement village. Girding my loins, I ventured to drive alone for more than two hours and to stay in a motel by myself for the first time. I enlisted the help of the proprietor to carry my bags from the car and negotiate my wheelchair up a step. I unpacked, ordered tea, and settled for the night, thrilled at this burst of independence. Enthusiastic prayers of thanks for safe arrival rose heavenward. What would the next day's adventure bring?

Travelling towards Gerringong the next morning, I was awestruck by the sparkling ocean on my left and the rolling green hills on my right. A rural girl at heart, I thought, "This is God's own country!"

When I arrived at the aged care facility, I was stunned by their generous hospitality. The clink of china cups and saucers and the finger-food presented in abundance made me feel like royalty. The CEO, the director of nursing, and the board members interviewed me in a friendly atmosphere. The questions were searching, and I had the impression they really wanted chaplaincy to work. They were not alone there! If they were motivated, I would pull out all stops. With my heart at peace, felt I had come home.

Positive relationships with my grandparents and previous experiences of chaplaincy coalesced at last in pastoral care with the ageing. A partnership with elderly people, their families, and the staff was cemented that day. I was impressed with the strong Christian ethos which undergirded the staff's care. Compassion for people was not just theoretical, but oozed out of their fingertips. When I inspected the home where I was to eventually hang my hat, I found the director of nursing with a tape measure in her hand, measuring my unit to see if my furniture would fit. Talk about servant leadership!

In sharing my excitement about the new ministry with our ministers' support group. I said, "Perhaps my slowness of movement, sometimes a disadvantage in a hurried society, is a gift to offer in pastoral care with ageing people."

10

Community Found

Third Ministry Placement
Home at Mayflower

A COSY UNIT in the independent living section of Mayflower Village became my home for the next eight years. The back windows looked over expansive green hills dotted with cows. I spotted the cottage that, as it happened, my parents had stayed in for their honeymoon over forty years before. I was struck by the strange cycles of life. Newly-wedded Mum and Dad never envisaged that their future daughter would be a chaplain at an aged care facility still to be erected in an adjacent paddock.

At night, I drifted off to sleep to the soothing sounds of whooshing ocean waves and the lowing of cattle. In the mornings I was greeted with rainbow lorikeets and playful sparrows. From the front door, I viewed the majestic Wedding Cake Mountain. This natural structure provided a spectacular backdrop to vividly coloured sunsets of red, grey, orange, and gold. My heart often leapt for joy as I praised the creative Master Artist, who I believed set up his easel, palette, and paintbrushes in this place of beauty.

Geographically, it suited me to live on the site of my work, because I did not have the effort of getting in and out of my car each day.

Another advantage was closer pastoral contact with residents, some of whom were my neighbours. The downside of that decision was that the boundaries between work and home life were blurry.

I bought a motorised wheelchair for the first time, to negotiate the big hills of Gerringong. I had to learn to tame this wild blue beast, complete with a bright orange flag flapping in the wind at the back to increase visibility. Any resemblance between riding a motorised chair and a wild bucking horse at a rodeo was purely coincidental. Perhaps it was just a matter of holding my mouth right while I had my learner plates on! Anyone who thinks that driving a motorised wheelchair is easy is a touch on the delusional side.

Work

My first public duty at Mayflower was to conduct a funeral—a new experience. I researched the history of the deceased centenarian lady. I had never met her, but I need not have worried.

The family gathered to grieve. *Grieve* was not exactly the right word though. The family wanted a celebratory atmosphere to mark her life. To my surprise, joy and tears of laughter surfaced as they reminisced together.

As another first, on my second day at the facility, I attended a dying man lying under the dim light of his bedside lamp. Sitting by his side was his eighty-year-old wife, white-haired and pint-sized. She was dressed in a bright red suit and striking red stockings. This loving widow was to become one of my most dedicated pastoral volunteers.

I also met Mollie, a resident with schizophrenia. I greeted her with "Hi, Mollie." Her raspy voice rattled without malice, "You bugger."

After my initial surprise, I thought, "I am going to love this place."

Occasionally, on request, I took my portable communion set with me to give Holy Communion to those who could not, for whatever reason, attend the sacrament during a church service. One such lady, whom I will call Miriam, was Greek Orthodox. She did not mind me, a Uniting Church minister, celebrating the sharing of bread and wine. We sat down at her dining table, on which were set the silver chalice of grape juice and the silver plate containing pieces of bread. I proceeded as reverently as I could to lead, using my order of service booklet.

Halfway through worship, which was not a long service, she interrupted to share, in a heavy Greek accent, her family history. At this point, I became aware of my former Presbyterian sensitivities, which encouraged me to conduct worship "decently and in order." Inwardly, I was startled, thinking she was rude to cut across a sacred ritual. However, I simply said out loud, "Miriam, I would love to hear your story after the service. Can we wait a bit?"

She stopped and I continued. Five minutes later, she interrupted again to recount a family memory. Again, I tried to redirect her energies, without success.

My Greek Orthodox friends may correct me if I am wrong, but at the back of my mind was a recollection of the Greek Orthodox liturgy at the World Council of Churches assembly. Amid the solemn chanting of the priests in the sanctuary, many of the congregants were talking about everyday events. I wondered whether Orthodox Christians saw no disrespect in joining the holy with the ordinary. Perhaps they put a high value on the priests, on whom they rely to tend to matters spiritual. Do they then feel comfortable in their own way to bring the ordinary into the divine Presence as well?

These first ministry opportunities could not have been more different from cataloguing books in the back room of a theological library. It was like jumping into the deep end, blindfolded.

I could not help but ponder the image of a mother eagle teaching her eaglet to fly. Firstly, she tips her offspring out of its nest to let it fall and flap. If the little one stumbles, she will fly under it to shelter it from free fall. Then she will leave it to its own devices to explore the joys and dangers of flying solo. I wondered at the time whether God, as mother eagle, had seriously overestimated my ability to launch into the deep in such a different ministry.

But Gerringong evolved into a challenging yet ultimately very fulfilling area of service. The mother eagle, though throwing me out of my comfort zone, never left me. In the joyful times and stretching moments to follow, my pastoral heart finally found a way to more fully express itself.

Fun and Refreshment

After strenuous workdays, I drove to Boat Harbour. This beachside scene became my regular haunt to restore temporary troubles to their eternal perspective. The timeless rhythm of the waves helped me regain my serenity.

On one occasion, a strong craving for a choc-coated ice cream enveloped me. On second thoughts, *enveloped* is too soft a word. More realistically, this addiction punched me in the face. I not only wanted ice cream, but needed it. I could not easily drive to the shops, get out of car, and go into the stores to buy it without tremendous physical effort. I prayed *hard*.

A few minutes later, a Mr Whippy ice cream van miraculously appeared on the scene. (I kid you not!) I beckoned the driver over from inside my car. I bought a choc-coated ice cream, and the driver handed it to me through my car window. Amazing! God is good in providing practical, everyday needs—even sugar fixes!

Occasionally, other opportunities to kick up my heels presented themselves. Thanks to the efforts of a local Member of Parliament, a number of people were invited to attend the opening ceremony of the Paralympic Games in Sydney in 2000. As one of the lucky guests, I cannot forget the electric, festive atmosphere enveloping the parade of athletes, who exhibited a wide range of (dis)abilities. Thunderous cheers barracked them on towards the sporting events of the next few days.

Normally a quiet person, I could not help but be scooped up in the spontaneous contagion of the event, yelling and screaming with the best of them. The vast audience bounced huge, brightly coloured balls across the crowd around the cavernous arena. We were united for a few hours in a celebration of triumph over adversity. This palpable spirit of exuberant fun could not be captured by watching the ceremony on television. You just had to be there.

Love and Wisdom from Catholic Friends

To escape temporarily from the helter-skelter life of pastoral care in a retirement village, this Protestant chaplain sometimes retreated to a Benedictine abbey nestled in the mountains of Jamberoo. I went for spiritual direction from the blue-habited Catholic nuns. Captivated by the sheer prayer-laden silence, majestic hills, and paddocks, I was drawn to the community's simple way of life. I loved browsing through their bookshop, attending their sung contemplative worship, and simply being lost in wonder as I gazed at the immensity of the landscape.

I was a grateful recipient of the nuns' friendly hospitality when my weary body and soul needed a Sabbath rest. Hospitality to the stranger is one of the tenets of the order. Chapter 53 of the Benedictine Rule states, "Let all guests who arrive be received like Christ, for he is going to say 'I came as a guest and you received me.' Matthew 25:35."[1] During gracious, laughing conversation over tea and muffins in a cosy dining room, I was privileged to meet widows who had chosen to become Benedictine nuns. Among their community also were former accountants, teachers, and university postgraduates.

My humour was tickled one day when I saw a nun perched on a tractor, rumbling around the grounds with veil folded back, her face flushed with exertion. The next minute, upon the ringing of the bell for chapel, she was serenely gliding into their beautiful sanctuary, eyes cast down and hands clasped as the community chanted their entry song.

I should not have been surprised at the apparent contradiction, because part of their Rule states:

> Idleness is the enemy of the soul.
> Therefore the sisters should be occupied
> at certain times in manual labour,
> and again at fixed hours in sacred reading.[2]

Their chaplain was Paul, a Carmelite priest and a musician-singer with whom I had dealings also as a fellow funeral celebrant. He sometimes visited his Catholic flock at Mayflower Gerringong, my pastoral patch. I spotted him there one time, bedecked in leather jacket and helmet. Seeing my speedy, motorized wheelchair and an intent look on my face, he smiled, saying "You look like a woman on a mission!"

As it was, I was on a deadline and momentarily irritated because my precious plan was interrupted. Then I remembered my manners. "Yes." I laughed. "Welcome, can I help you find somebody you might be looking for?"

"As a matter of fact, yes. Can you direct me to Mrs So-and-So's room?"

My brain shifted gear. I abandoned my deadline, stopped, and did a U-turn in the direction of the desired destination. We reached the room, only to find nobody at home. Foiled, Paul decided to abandon looking further, and I proceeded to escort him back to where he had parked his bike.

Paul's eyes sparkled as they rested upon a garden of colourful bronze and purple pansies in our courtyard. I was still in "hurry" mode, anxious to get back to get back to my original agenda. Paul, on the other hand was in "slow" mode. I thought, "Doesn't Paul know I have an important task to do?"

He bent down to the garden, breathed deeply, and touched the flowers gently. Focusing on the deep purple pansies particularly, he exclaimed, "How beautiful!"

Grudgingly, I admitted he was absolutely right. The innocent pansy faces smiled up at us in their regal splendour. I softened.

He continued, "Did you realise that, according to Gestalt spirituality, the colour purple symbolises the presence of the King within you?" (For Christians, "the King" is Christ. We celebrate the coming of the King in Advent by decorating our churches in the colour purple).

My heart stopped still. In my agitated speed to complete my to-do list, I realised that I had almost lost sight of the beauty that was right in front of us. It was not just the exquisiteness of the pansies, but the deeper insight of the King's presence within us right there and then. This was surely a grace-filled moment. I hoped after that epiphany to be interrupted more often.

This was not the end of the story. I shared the incident with a friend of mine. Months later, she presented me with a beautiful, multicoloured patchwork quilt of reds, greens, yellows, and—you guessed it—purples. Interspersed among the coloured squares are vibrant images of purple pansies.

Patchwork quilts are a creative medium of sewing the threads of a person's life story together. Fifteen years later, the quilt is keeping my knees warm now as I write—a crafted reminder of the King's presence within me.

Relationships with Directors of Nursing

I was privileged to serve with three directors of nursing during my eight years at Mayflower. All were inspirational in their leadership, providing fine examples of compassion to elderly residents and their families. They each contributed to my growth. How? I would like to share two examples.

As a conscientious soul, I was often overwhelmed by the residents' continuous need and felt unable to meet it. One director advised me, "You don't have to fix it all. If possible, your conversation gives residents and staff the energy to take the next step." This insight helped to rein in my Messiah complex, which could easily have burnt me out.

I read about a minister who offered a complementary insight. "You are not Jesus. You just need to put in a good word for him occasionally."[3]

The same director was of Irish Catholic descent. His spirituality often added sparkle to my serious Scottish heritage. One of my responsibilities was to lead worship services a couple of times a week in the aged care facility. My style tended to be simple, reverent, ordered, and disciplined. Sometimes he said to me, "My Catholic heritage has a lot of feast days and holy days. We celebrate with abandon. Don't be afraid to celebrate your Uniting Church anniversaries and so on. We can always organise a cake to add joy to the occasion."

Palliative Care

Palliative care, in partnership with other members of the health team, was a special part of my ministry. Being with dying people and their families, whether they were people of faith or not, was for me like standing on sacred ground. I sometimes felt that the staff and I were midwives to the dying person, ushering them into the next phase of new life.

The reactions of loved ones to death and the dying process were different each time. Some relatives sat in stunned silence, clearly ill at ease and unable to find words. Some struggled with family conflict which had surfaced. For many, chatty reminiscence about good times past seemed to fit like a glove. Another sat solo, quietly knitting to keep her loved one company in her last hours. Yet others read Scripture and sang hymns.

For residents who had no family, the staff took special care to come in, greet them, attend to their health needs, and even plant a kiss on their foreheads. It was my role to sit with residents, staff, and family, to love them through their difficult vigils, and to listen carefully to stories shared. Sometimes I prompted people to speak directly to their family member, even though the resident was seemingly unconscious. The sense of hearing is the last sense to remain during life.

In one particularly demanding winter at Mayflower, about seventeen palliative residents died over the course of three weeks. To say I was exhausted would be an understatement. In order to recover my sanity, I lumbered uptown to treat myself to a remedial massage. While my body was draped like thinly rolled pastry over the table in blissful oblivion, my mobile phone rang to let me know that Person 17 was dying. I cut the massage session short, scraped my drooping body off the bed with a spatula, and hot-wheeled it down the hill to the retirement village again.

Many people look at me strangely when I say that I gain satisfaction from conducting funerals. It is an honour to help families plan their goodbyes. Their stories of the person remembered are often fascinating. I find myself wishing I had known this particular fabric of a resident's life when they were alive. What conversations we could have had! I sometimes felt sad that I only knew these people at a fragile part of their journey—but then again, what a privilege to accompany them in their more mellow years.

One funeral I conducted was a burial in a cemetery overlooking a magnificent view of the ocean. The camber of the ground sloped steeply, and the burial plot was precariously near the edge of a cliff. The brakes on my wheelchair were not as secure as they could have been. I asked the funeral director whether I could borrow his foot to jam against my wheel. He happily obliged, thus preventing an unexpected exiting dive from the chaplain! Funeral directors have a varied job description. On another occasion, I celebrated my birthday by conducting two funerals in the one day.

One of the challenges and privileges of working with ageing people is growing to love them deeply and then surrendering them to the mercy of God as they near the end of their earthly journey. I found goodbyes difficult, even though for many, death was a blessed release from suffering.

The other skill I needed to develop was welcoming new residents with the joy and reassurance they deserved. They were often occupying the same bed as a person to whom I had just said farewell, sometimes as recently as the day before. Those who work in chaplaincy require responsive emotional elasticity, so that it is possible to "Rejoice with those who rejoice; mourn with those who mourn." (Rom. 12:15 NIV)

In addition to debriefing well after deaths, I found it important to receive with open hands God's gift of each resident who came through the door. "Love deeply, but hold lightly, because I do not possess them" were words I said to myself often. These beloved people were only on loan to me, to care for and nurture for a limited time.

Different Forms of Ministry

The major thrust of my ministry at Gerringong was pastoral care—sitting alongside people in joys and grief, and conducting church services and funerals. However, sometimes my vocational journey took unusual twists.

The local council once asked me to lead a dedication service for restored dry stone walls, which provided boundaries for lush green paddocks. My prayer books did not include such rituals, so creativity and research into the historical function of the walls was needed for me to rise to the occasion.

The debutante ball was a regular event on the rural calendar. Elegantly dressed young women and their penguin-suited escorts were presented to a pillar of society. I had never seen myself as a "pillar" before, but I nevertheless enjoyed the different experience, giving a pep talk at the local town hall.

Christian devotional sessions took place in many settings. The most unusual was in a Snoezelen room. (Snoezelen is a Dutch word pronounced SNOO-zlen.) It was a quiet, multi-sensory room where small groups of people with dementia, or people who were highly agitated, could come for relaxation. By use of a special projector, slow-moving, swirling, abstract images in pastel colours were projected onto the four walls for residents to focus on. Soft music was played. Sometimes Christian messages were shared against this backdrop. Other times, the images and music spoke for themselves. The ultimate aim was to provide a safe space for troubled residents to be soothed and enveloped by love.

Worship can engage all senses, not just hearing. For people with dementia, whose language skills are challenged by their condition, sight can add joy and vibrancy in the experience of God. Two of my creative friends helped me lead worship one Sunday. They were gifted in liturgical dance, using their bodies and colourful ribbons to bring Scripture and prayer alive in graceful movement. On another occasion, I invited a Christian theatre group to enact plays with a strong message, to add zest to our worship service.

11

Leading Through Others

Fourth Ministry Placement

AFTER A PERIOD, I began to feel stale, as if I had nothing more to give the Mayflower community. One day, an intriguing formal-looking letter poked out from my mail pigeonhole. I tore the envelope open, to find that it was from a chaplain friend. He was serving on a recruitment committee looking for a replacement chaplain in a Central Coast set of aged care facilities. The committee was still searching for a person after a one-year vacancy. Would I consider the position? I must have read through the typewritten epistle about six times.

Something stirred within me, big time. My hands started to shake, my cheeks flushed, and my heart pumped like choofing pistons on a steam engine. In my former secular employment, I had never been headhunted. I had always had to chase employment avenues. To be offered the opportunity to apply for a position was a new experience and a massage to my little ego.

Once the initial excitement died down, though, my rational brain kicked in. I had physical support systems carefully in place at Mayflower, a cosy home, the benefit of a strong community, and supportive employers. Why would I want to change? To re-establish myself in a new environment with adequate support would be a challenge of monolithic proportions. I am not usually a person who relishes change. I can be a regular stick in the mud.

I waited a day or two to see if there were any divine nudges to guide me. My sense of excitement grew at the possibility of a new venture. I believed that if God was guiding me, he would give me strength to let go of a beloved community and begin again.

I decided to further test the calling by putting in a job application and seeing how God would work. An interview was granted, so with my heart in my mouth, I travelled to the Central Coast. I faced a group of five or six people, some of whom looked a bit formidable. Their foreheads were creased in serious furrows, and the atmosphere was distinctly earnest. Their questions were searching, and I was not at all sure whether they would accept me for the position.

However, for some reason they did. They mentioned in passing that I had the warm personality for which they were looking. Their positive response was another confirmation of my new calling.

Saying goodbye to "my" flock at Gerringong, however, was one of the hardest hurdles I have had to jump. I burst into tears at my farewells. To this day, I remember getting into my car for the last time there, flanked with family support. My shoulders slumped forward and I sobbed. Pastoral relationships have a sneaky way of entangling themselves around tender hearts. The deeper the connection, the more vulnerable are the feelings. Ministry and its associated moves are not without their cost.

As we travelled to my new place of ministry, I felt literally homeless. I related well to the old song "Mr In-Between." It was true that there was a house which had been modified for my needs. Building changes had been negotiated through phone contact, emails, and floor plans. But I had never actually seen the results. Talk about an exercise in faith!

I need not have worried. The house was comfortable, light and airy. The accurate measurements by the renovators enabled my wheelchair to fit comfortably.

Delight with the house was quickly followed by a meteoric thud into reality when I nervously launched into work. I seriously wanted to leave after the second day—a rather devastating conclusion at which to arrive. The only reason I found to stay was all the trouble my family had taken to move me.

I found the corporate culture very different from the rural community spirit of Gerringong. The pace of work and life seemed much faster, and initially more impersonal. In those first days, I felt like a scurrying ant under an elephant's foot. My employer required statistics for pastoral care, written accountability, and greater use of the computer for communication. What a joyful surprise it was when a power outage encouraged staff to come to my office to talk in person rather than emailing.

I yearned for the nurturing community spirit of my former facility, and wished for more one-on-one contact with the new staff. At the end of the day, I sat like a stunned mullet, trying to process the chaos in my mind. In a desperate effort to cling to the comfort of the past, I would often say to those gracious enough to listen, "We always did it this way at Gerringong." With the benefit of hindsight, I see that this was not the most helpful public observation to make.

One of the challenges was ministering with a much wider population. I realised fast that I was not a solo chaplain, but a team leader of four and, later, even more pastoral care workers and volunteers. A new skill set was required. Personalities were different and job allocations complicated. I discovered that management was the ability to achieve objectives through others. Whereas before I had done the majority of pastoral care myself, now I learned the art of delegation. Trust in my team was required. To some extent, I had to take my hands off the piano keys and allow the pianola to play its own music.

Communication among staff and residents over numerous facilities was a skill I had to master. In addition, I had never had to recruit and harness a professional team before. My learning curve was incredibly steep.

Despite my novice efforts, I can say that our pastoral teams, for all their diversity, were very dedicated over the years. Leadership, I discovered, was sacrificial. I needed to open my eyes to the needs and gifts of my team and let go of previously loved tasks to enable others to develop their skills.

For all the personal challenges, there were big pluses. The first CEO I worked with on the Central Coast was a visionary who prized innovation and believed in trusting his people to make decisions within their circle of influence. My ability to take responsibility developed over time. Reading books on leadership and team building was of great assistance.

One of qualities I appreciated about the leader was his encouragement of staff to make leaps of faith in new directions, saying, "It is better to ask forgiveness than to ask permission." Within this culture, the pastoral care department instituted a programme of aromatherapy for a time. Another ministry evolved for visiting people with disability and mental illness in their homes. We also ran carer support groups to offer skilled friendship to the relatives of ageing people as they cared for their loved ones, whether in residential care or in the community. Conducting numerous worship services was also an important part of our work.

Staff restructures were relatively commonplace over the twelve years I spent in this position, requiring flexibility in adapting to ever-new policies and personnel changes. Each director brought his own style to the mix. For all the changes, an amazing creativity flowed to make way for new trends in the delivery of aged care.

One of the blessings of working on the Central Coast was the team-work of my three chaplaincy leader colleagues who worked in other geographical areas. Chaplaincy can at times be isolating. Some people misunderstand our role, believing we are "Holy Joes who have no earthly use." To get together with others who knew the intricacy and diversity that the job entailed was a godsend. We were not called the Three Amigos for nothing! In those group times, I discovered the reality of the slogan of our aged care organisation: "Together, Stronger."

Yet another joy was to provide opportunities for pastoral care students, volunteers, and pastoral staff to gain exposure and learning in an aged care setting. While supervising new kids on the block could sometimes be demanding, the overwhelming positive was the knowledge that I was investing in their futures. If I could engender a new sense of vocation in people wanting to enter the aged care profession, then I was happy. Sowing seeds of satisfaction and skill in others gave me hope beyond the present.

The ability to work through these teams was vital for my role, but my first and enduring love was face-to-face pastoral contact with residents. I often felt extraordinarily privileged to sit alongside them as they coped with ever-increasing limitation, family concerns, navigation through the welfare system, and the myriad other relationship issues that arise through community living. To conduct their funerals was an honour. To discover the richness of their stories in life and in death was an experience I will never forget.

Tall Trees

While serving on a disability advisory committee for UnitingCare Ageing Central Coast, I became captivated by the vision of a committee member who was a parent of a young adult with an intellectual disability. As a primary teacher, she wanted to form a recreation club for young people with disability. Eventually, we were able to put legs on the dream.

The clientele for the club included people who were residents of disability group homes run by UnitingCare. Activities for the club, called Tall Trees because of the beauty of the stately gum trees surrounding the property, were varied. With the help of volunteers, we offered a Christian devotional programme, personal sharing, cooking, hospital art, gardening, comedy, computer education, and occasional outings for picnics, movies, and the like. For five years, this programme provided fun and education for enthusiastic participants with intellectual disabilities.

Coaching

At this stage, I met with a personal coach, who enabled people to set and achieve goals to enhance their quality of life. My personal life needed a kick-start to add enthusiasm and verve. With the coach's help, I set achievable, concrete goals.

One objective was to secure my financial future. I wanted to purchase an investment property for provision of rental income. After setting out clear steps to achieve this goal, I reached for the finishing line with all my might. Imagine my delight when, years later, the mortgage on my villa was finally discharged, complete with a secure tenant. Bells, whistles, and streamers exploded in my mind to celebrate. The quality of my personal life improved.

Professionally, following a planned review of my ministry on the Central Coast, I realised that unless I made changes, I was headed for burnout. I was a diligent worker, but at times I could not see the wood for the trees in what was a huge job. My employers funded the professional coach primarily to support me through necessary adjustments to my job and to teach me the skills of team leadership.

Using the underpinning of the positive psychology movement, the coach assessed my personality style and strengths to help define coping strategies. His friendship and guidance were invaluable. I had to develop the ability to get work done through others, trusting them rather than continually checking up on them.

In addition, it is a requirement that Uniting Church ministers in placement have a mentor with whom to meet regularly. This person facilitates reflection on the practice of Christian ministry and theology. Throughout my almost thirty years of ordained ministry, I have been blessed to sit with wise ministers who have shared their experience with me.

Hospitals

In the midst of work management challenges, which I was addressing with welcome assistance, my body was developing osteoarthritis on top of my pre-existing physical conditions. Early one morning, I was woken by the insistent buzzing of the alarm clock. I reached over sleepily to turn the noise off. Unfortunately, I knocked the clock to the floor, under the bed and out of my reach. It was still screaming its head off. Slowly, I sat up on the side of the bed and proceeded to a kneeling position on the floor. The clock was still beyond the reach of my fingers.

Resigned to the continuous assault on my eardrums, I tried to heave myself back on the bed. My knees and shoulders were sore, and I simply did not have the strength. I rang for an ambulance. The paramedics' help in getting me afloat was appreciated, but I realised I had further damaged my shoulders and knee.

I continued to wage battle with pain, faithfully going to work, but I was reaching the end of my rope. One morning, I felt like a stiff tin soldier. Seeing my contorted face in the bathroom mirror, I prayed earnestly to God, "Show me what to do. I cannot stand the agony any longer."

I inched my way to the car to drive to work, aware that I had to take devotions. I attempted to transfer from my motorised wheelchair to my car, but couldn't lift myself high enough to reach the car seat. My knee and shoulders were so sore, I could not move. I was stuck. In desperation, I phoned 000 for an ambulance, from the mobile phone hanging around my neck.

When the officers arrived, they took me to the local public hospital. On the one hand, I was scared. On the other, I was relieved that someone could look after me and give me the right treatment.

Who could forget the kindness of the female intern doctor who held my hand as I sobbed through the intensity of a pain I ranked at 11 on a scale of 10? She and a nurse must have been my strong advocates to the pressured emergency doctor, who wanted to send me home. The doctor prescribed me a very strong pain killer. For the first time in months, I became pain-free, which was a blissful relief.

However, in just a few minutes I almost became unconscious, putting the attending staff in a mild panic. They quickly lowered me to a flat position in the electric bed. It seemed that I was allergic to the drug. After X-rays, they admitted me to hospital. I believe this was God's answer to my earnest prayer that morning.

During the hospital stay, I discovered the wonders of medically prescribed steroids. Walking pain-free with a spring in my step and little energy expenditure was a cause for great celebration. I moved with the momentum of a Puffing Billy train. I did not realise at the time the possible dangerous side effects of the drug. In keeping with recommended practice, the medical team reduced the dose. My pain returned, and I was introduced to morphine skin patches.

After what seemed like an eternity, I was transferred to a private hospital for intensive rehabilitation. The honeymoon of novelty soon wore off. Time stood still. Feelings of fear, frustration and stuckness were my constant companions. I did not mind the hard slog of physio, but the dark cloud of uncertainty about my physical deterioration and the threat of transition from independent living to residential care hung over me. A couple of grim-faced, military-like staff did nothing to build my confidence. My medically supervised experimentation with different painkillers often left me in deep states of stupor.

My terror was softened by a skilled rehabilitation specialist and some hand-picked, compassionate nurses. One lent me music to play in a quiet moment. Its Christian words, "One day at a time," helped to calm my spirit. On another occasion, the same nurse answered my phone to an unsuspecting caller by using the greeting "Heather's private secretary." Her humour lubricated the ruggedly screeching wheels of my hospital experience.

There were other moments of grace—gifts of God—in the struggle. Who could forget the faithfulness of pastoral care visitors from my church, who nourished me with strawberry milkshakes? I was moved by visits from my faithful mum, family, and friends. There was a phone call from my eldest nephew to share the exciting news of his engagement. The jokes made by the Scottish husband of my hospital roommate tickled my sense of humour.

While my usual specialist was on leave, there was a concerted push to move me from living at home to residential care—a terrifying thought. Having worked in aged care, I knew too much about the dangers of institutionalisation. There were very few, if any, accommodation alternatives for younger people like myself with higher support needs. The hospital social worker told me later that she was avoiding me during that period, not wanting to discuss the tough residential care transition.

Six weeks into the hospital stay and becoming stir-crazy, I fantasized about staging my escape. In my dreams, I stripped my bedclothes, knotted them together, and abseiled from my hospital window.

Eventually, once community care hours were added to my package, fantasy became reality and I returned home. I was out of condition from being in hospital, and for a while was physically weak. The emotional recovery from the ordeal took longer. Nonetheless, being home in familiar surroundings and regaining personal empowerment again was wonderfully therapeutic. My employers were kind enough to arrange a staged return to work. With the assistance of physios, carers, and family, my life returned to my normal for a year—until the next dip in the road.

Reflecting on this hospital experience, my sister-in-law Carolyn observed, "It took the health professionals a long time to be convinced that you needed hospitalisation at first. Then it took them even longer to be persuaded you could cope at home. They probably underestimated your abilities."

The Parable of the Jacaranda

To celebrate my discharge from hospital, two girlfriends and I holidayed in a rural town bedecked in purple jacaranda trees. Each of us bought a jacaranda sapling as a memento of our trip. When I returned home, one of the girls accompanied me to a nearby hardware store to buy fertiliser and a spade. Armed with these items, we planted my specimen in the front yard with due ceremony.

The symbolism of "my" jacaranda assumed great power. It became an icon of my physical and emotional recovery from a long stint in hospital. For a while my little tree flourished. Then frost, storm, and root difficulties challenged its very existence. In its stress, it defoliated and suffered many "bad hair" days. It has been lovingly tended with nutrients, water, and gentle whispers of encouragement by its nurturing owner, her mother, and her gardener. Five years down the track, it is still alive.

My dream of a towering, stately living organism, giving shelter to all who would pass by, is yet to be realised. Many would laugh at this pitiful excuse of a plant. However, after steady rainfall, it is now looking the best it ever has.

When I travelled to Brisbane, Queensland, most of the jacarandas I saw were huge, graceful, and flourishing with lavender blossom. I was tempted to take a photograph of one breathtaking specimen to show it to my plant partner in the struggle. I would like to say, "Hello, friend. This is what you can aspire to if you keep going. Have a look and be encouraged. This is what you will look like when you grow up!"

I have been nudged by those around me to think that the recovery of the battling shrub does not equate with the reality of my own progress. However, my gutsy little green companion is still an inspiration to me. We share one great quality in common—perseverance in the face of mighty difficulty. There is a strange sense of solidarity in our mutual wrestling for a meaningful existence. Who says there cannot be a strong connection between the plant and human kingdoms?

Another Private Hospital—2010

In the interim period between hospital visits, I experimented with Botox injections in my adductor muscles, under the supervision of a neurologist. I hoped Botox would loosen the tight muscles in that area, thus making my walking easier.

Unfortunately, one of the side effects of the treatment is that the targeted muscles lose their strength for a period. Consequently, when I practised walking alone along the hallway at home, as part of my exercise regime, I found it more difficult to turn around and get back into my wheelchair from a standing position unsupervised. Consequently, I found myself on the floor more often than not. Ambulance officers were faithful in coming to my rescue, until I concluded that my days of unsupervised walking were over.

I theorised that my frequent falls during that stage contributed to increased malformation of my knee and ankle joints. This challenge, combined with increasing shoulder strain, gradually pointed to the need for another stint in hospital, but not before the following incidents.

A long drive to a rural work commitment, during which I became hopelessly lost, damaged my already sore shoulders even more. Upon arrival home, I couldn't even lift the key to unlock my front door. I called for nearby help. Next morning, I scared myself witless because it took me half an hour to get out of bed, due to excruciating pain. I realised I could not look after myself at home.

I called my GP, who made a home visit. My tears of frustration and fear flowed easily in his presence. We both realised I needed to go to hospital. Bless him. As a Christian, he prayed for me. I was very moved by his compassion.

I mentioned that I did not want a long hospital stay, simply enough to get me rested and then functioning again. He was able to admit me the very next day to a different local private hospital. On the day of my departure by ambulance, I was surprisingly calm. An intensive rehabilitation programme of physio and hydrotherapy was set in train.

This rehabilitation unit was a happy place, with great morale among the staff. However, my new rehabilitation specialist steeled my intense determination to prove his prognosis wrong. Near the end of my stay, he confidently pronounced, "Next time you go to hospital, you will end up in residential care."

"Over my dead body," I thought, as I inwardly bristled. Thoughts of a being a person in her late fifties, living for thirty years in institutional residential aged care, in a four-bed ward alongside people with severe memory loss, raced chaotically through my head. I asked out loud, "How long ahead do you think that would be?" He said, "Two years."

It is six years later at the time of writing. With the help of my GP, wonderful community physio, and faithful community care workers, I am still living alone at home. However, I have no illusions that I could survive without a willing group of people around me. As they say in the classics, "No man is an island."

Before I left hospital, the reality of my arthritic shoulders led to a tough question as to whether I could ever drive again. I burst into tears at the prospect of a further loss of independence. However, with the assistance of an occupational therapist and my mum, further driving and car seat modifications were arranged.

I was still able to drive short distances of less than half an hour, and used wheelchair taxis a lot more. I grew in affection for the wonderful band of regular drivers who, with the use of half-price taxi vouchers, extended my working life by transporting me to places I would not otherwise have been able to go.

I returned to work for another four years, having stabilised my pain, before finally hanging up my chaplaincy hat.

12

Salute To People Who Are Ageing: Partners In Life

WHAT HAS A chapter on ageing people to do with an autobiography on disability? All I can say is that for twenty years of my working life, I have been in their company. They have an endearing habit of getting under my skin. The lessons I have learned from people nearing the end of their life cycle have often given me food for thought. Here are snippets of life in an aged care facility, which changed the way I look at older people. They help me realise that the challenges of ageing and of disability do have many similarities.

Need for Meaning

An image that has haunted me through the years is of a red-haired lady with gold-rimmed glasses perched precariously on her nose. In her nineties, she was sitting alone, downcast, in the auditorium of an aged care facility. Her shoulders slumped. I struck up conversation.

She intoned slowly, "I am bored and I want to feel useful. Is there anything I can do to help?"

Here she was, still yearning to make a contribution. She had been a busy wife and mum in the past. Now, seemingly, no one needed her any more.

My heart reached out to her. My immediate reaction was to go into fix-it mode. My mind raced through possibilities. Could she roll bandages for the nurses? Could she fold clothes? Could she set the table?

My brain sometimes veers to the negative. Unless I train it correctly, it is like a car needing a wheel alignment. Internally, I picked a thousand reasons as to why those solutions would not work—Wellbeing, Health, and Safety requirements, time restriction, her own physical challenges. The list went on.

Looking back on the conversation now, I realise I short-changed her. My creativity was stunted by my own time-pressured deadlines. At the very least, I could have engaged her in a longer conversation about her quest for meaning.

Perhaps as we age, it is not necessarily the number of tasks we complete in a day that matters, but our capacity to continue to connect with people in a meaningful way. In addition, it is still vital to have a sense of purpose which is greater than ourselves. For myself as a Christian, a relationship with the divine is important, but for others it could be a love of nature, art, or culture. Ageing with some degree of contentment requires a transition from a lifestyle of frenetic doing to an attitude of being.

Being issues may tumble through our minds. "Am I comfortable to be around?" "Are there still small kindnesses I can share with those around me?" "What kind of legacy (not just money) do I want to leave?" "How can I best share of my experience with the younger generation?" "Is there anything I have left to arrange, so that others may breathe a little more easily?" "Is there anyone I need to forgive?" "How can I nourish my inner life to prepare for my death and life to come?"

Gordon B. Hinckley, aged ninety-two, hits the nail on the head:

> I am no longer a young man filled with energy and vitality. I'm given to meditation and prayer. I would enjoy sitting in a rocker, swallowing prescriptions, listening to soft music, and contemplated the things of the universe. But such activity offers no challenge and makes no contribution and purpose. I wish to use every waking hour to give encouragement, to bless those whose burdens are heavy, to build faith and strength of testimony. It is the presence of wonderful people which stimulates the adrenalin. It is the look of love in their eyes that gives me energy.[1]

An aged care lifestyle coordinator I once knew instituted a wonderful programme of linking the local schoolchildren with selected residents of an aged care facility. As well as meeting up occasionally at the facility or the school, the buddies wrote messages of encouragement, telling their respective stories to each other in an exercise book which flew to and fro between their places of living and education. To me that was an exciting initiative to cross the generational boundaries and to nurture a positive sense of contribution at both ends of the life cycle.

Need for Contact

One of the many things about which I get passionate is the strong need for family members and friends to keep regular contact with their older loved ones. It is tempting to think that once ageing relatives move into a facility, then all their needs will be met. It can be an excuse for cutting some tricky ties altogether.

I am the first to admit that family relationships can be convoluted at times. Some relatives can drive us crackers. But unless these connections are destructive, then continuing contact can be therapeutic for healthy ageing. Many a time, I have known residents to stay in their rooms, declining to join activities in the event that a family member "might" just come and visit.

Loneliness is one of the big challenges of ageing. Lack of mobility and the severing of people connections can contribute to isolation. Families are now more far-flung than in former days. Many cannot pop round the corner for a chat because they live interstate. But even the kindest of staff and the innovation of recreational programming is no substitute for old friends and family. They are the ones who often know an aged person's history most intimately.

Don't Judge a Book by Its Cover

As clearly as the day is long, I remember a very frail lady, bedridden, with no speech. At first I did not know what to say to her, given she could not respond. When I found my voice, I spoke words of simple love. I stroked her hair and forehead. A moment later, I saw tears fall from her eyes. I was overwhelmed and completely undone. Here was not simply a withered body in a bed, but a fellow human being, no less a child of God.

On another occasion, I encountered an aged care resident. She had the reputation of being cranky, out of sorts, and bitter. We talked for a while about very ordinary things. Then, out of the blue, she burst into tears. It was if the dam had burst and the floodgates had opened. The years have obliterated for me what the nature of her grief was, except to say that it involved her struggle to care for her sister and mother. How easy it is for me to make snap judgements about people with crusty exteriors. Behind a tough facade, there is often a hurting heart. I realised the truth of the wisdom I had heard on another occasion: "Pastoral care can be likened, on occasions, to holding a baby in your arms as she/he throws a tantrum."[2]

Blessings of Ageing

I met another elderly Christian lady at dusk, sitting on a park bench situated within the grounds of the retirement village. She was gazing with a far-away look in her eyes at a brilliantly coloured sunset framing a mountain. I greeted her, a woman of exquisite gentleness and contentment. Her words wove their faithfulness into my soul. She murmured, "Old age is a benediction."

For many years I had listened to words of frustration about the trials of getting older, but what a gift she shared with me that day. She did not enlarge as to why old age was a blessing. I saw what she meant with my own eyes. Old age, with its enforced slowness, enables the possibility of contemplating deeply the sheer beauty around us.

Losses of Ageing

There is beauty, definitely, in a retirement village, but there is also suffering. Dementia can be a cruel disease. It robs people of memory, planning ability, and language skills. One woman I grew to love had faithfully nursed her mum through dementia over a long period of time. I was speaking with this now-elderly daughter in a public meeting area of the nursing home. She too had become a resident in a wheelchair.

In the course of our conversation, her eyes reddened and the tears welled up. I asked what was troubling her. She replied "My mum had dementia, and now I am starting to forget too. I don't like the way my mind is going. I am getting confused. I know I am getting dementia too, and I hate it!"

Words fail me at times like this. I could not offer false hope and say, "You are imagining it." She of all people knew the implications of her disease. I could not say, "You will be all right," because her condition was going to rob her of some of her capacities.

All I could say through my listening, my words, and my touch was that we would love her through it.

I find the initial stages of dementia particularly painful because the one suffering still has insight into their possible future. Further down the track, when insight has faded, the particular grief of knowledge lessens. It is the carers and family members who feel the sadness of loss of the person they once knew.

Not Forgotten in Ageing

One of the questions which bubbled in my mind occasionally was related to people with dementia. With cognitive function gradually declining and memories disappearing, how is a person's spirituality to be supported?

Two things I knew through reading and personal observation were that long-term memory is one of the last functions to deteriorate, and that appreciation of music also remains for a long time. So reminiscing about someone's experience in their early church or Sunday school life (if they were a person of faith) was sometimes helpful. Playing hymns which they may have learned at a young age could occasionally prompt them to sing or tap their feet. Music resonates in a way that plain words do not.

What happens when a person of deep spirituality "forgets" that they believed in God? Sometimes physical symbols like crosses or Bibles can trigger memory. Through all of this experience, though, I am encouraged by the comforting words of God's grace in the prophet Isaiah:

Can a mother forget the baby at her breast and have no compassion on the child she has borne? Though she may forget, I will not forget you! See, I have engraved you on the palms of my hands; your walls are ever before me. (Isa. 49:15–16 NIV)

Diversity in Ageing

It is sometimes tempting to look at a community of grey-haired, bespectacled, hard of hearing, visually impaired older people en masse, and make blanket assumptions about how people age. How wrong can we be!

I have known people in their nineties who vigorously walk around the corridors as if their lives depended on it. There are others in their sixties whose bodies battle with simple movement. Some have a complaining attitude, yet others with more to whinge about are a breath of fresh air when it comes to positive attitude. Some women have developed a strong sense of identity through raising a family. Others still recall their working-career successes with great pride. Some possess a wicked sense of humour. Others are straight as a die, never daring to crack a smile. Some have narrow boundaries in their lives. Others have hearts and minds as big as Texas.

To get to know each person as an individual is one of the great challenges of working with ageing people. What a rainbow of colour there is!

Creativity in Ageing

Those of us who work or live with people who are ageing have a responsibility to encourage continuing creativity.

To illustrate: One of the highlights of taking devotional services in a dementia unit was my contact with a man I'll call Adam. In his seventies, contending with a lifelong condition of intellectual disability, he attended church regularly, armed with a well-worn Bible. Each week he would show me in his gentle, kind manner some of his writings, carefully crafted in black ink. Some were letters addressed to various politicians, sharing his simple wisdom about how to overcome the problems of the world. Most of his work, though, took the form of coloured pencil drawings, often depicting childlike figures from famous Bible stories.

Sadly, all his family had predeceased him. But it was heart-warming to see how the staff encouraged him. They continued to supply him with artistic materials so that his inner imagination could still splash onto the page.

Respect and Dignity in Ageing

As a recipient of care myself, I am particularly sensitive to the need to preserve dignity. Just because a person is advanced in years is no excuse for workers being lax in their sensitivity of communication. The query "Have you had your bowels open today?" yelled at the top of one's voice amid others, can redden faces. For the health professional to assume the ageing resident knows nothing of their care regime can also be demeaning. Communicating from "above" to "below," without recognition of talking and listening among equals, is annoying at best, disempowering at worst. The use of words such as *dearie*, *sweetie*, and *darling*, however well meant, can be patronising.

We need to value the ageing person's history and contribution to our community. Some have been scientists, police officers, teachers, nurses, artists, inventors, soldiers, or spies. Do not let wrinkled faces trick you into underestimating the value of their service. Their reminiscences are often a great source of wisdom. Resilience and mental toughness over periods of great social change are to be admired.

Playfulness in Ageing

Occasionally residents had me in stitches. On one festive dining occasion, a retired ambulance officer pulled an object out of his pocket and placed it carefully on a crisply ironed white tablecloth in front of me. It was a plastic toy set of lifelike false teeth. The battery-operated dentures started chattering and clacking of their own accord around the table. I could not stop laughing. Old age is no excuse for denying your inner child.

13

Retirement: A Change of Pace

ACCORDING TO ECCLESIASTES, there is a time for everything—a season for holding on and letting go (3:1–7.) I had poured myself into my work and given it my best shot.

But now it was time to take a more restful sojourn. The decision to retire was not a decision to stop, but to change pace and direction. My body, mind, and spirit yearned for the pillow of relaxation.

I have a dislike of being bored and still have a strong need to contribute, using the gifts with which I have been blessed. However, exercising more choice in doing and resting was and is delightful.

Closure of Ministry Service

My farewells and closure of ministry church service were heart-warming celebrations. Many gathered to say goodbye. During the service, my ritual handing back of the symbols of ministry—the Bible, wine and bread, pastoral visiting lists—was a powerful reminder to me of handing over the mantle of pastoral care to my successors. The work of God continues, despite the changing of the guard.

My brother Mal was unable to be at the service. However, he sent this moving email. My tears of appreciation flowed. I quote in part:

> You must be processing many memories today as you think back over your many years in active ministry. Many highs and lows, many frustrations and some joys too. Many difficult people and some lovely people. Church structures which don't work well, and some that are sometimes helpful. Engagement with retreats and resources which are challenging and sometimes water for a thirsty soul. Days and nights when you struggle to come up with something significant to say in a sermon, or times when you have been inspired and touched by a little comment or deed by someone else. Aha moments. Times when God seems a long way away and the odd sunrise moments of closeness or awe. Trying to recover from hurts and mistakes and times of appreciating the grace of God. Times of difficulty getting to and from work. Finding yourself stuck on the floor of the car, times when the carer didn't show up, times when other people didn't show or didn't or weren't allowed to help. Times when people parked in your spot. Times when it was just such a hassle or pain to get to work. Times when people are actually helpful. Times when you had to spend those days in hospital. You have experienced a lot.

The thing that always inspires me is your faithfulness and dogged determination. I haven't finished preparing my sermon… but I was wondering whether I may include some of your story of faithfulness to the God who pushes and shoves and yet oddly at the same time carries us gently to places unfamiliar, challenging and unknown.

I know this is a transition point. You are not finishing your ministry today, but it is a significant point in your life and I know you have many questions about the future. I wish you, and pray for, every blessing for today and then for the rest of your life in ministry.

Thank you for being an inspiration and thank you for your faithful and hard-working example.

Well done good and faithful servant!

I know it's a bit of a cliché but maybe at this point it is a good time to reflect on Psalm 23.

> The LORD is my shepherd, I lack nothing. He makes me lie down in green pastures, he leads me beside quiet waters, he refreshes my soul.
>
> He guides me along the right paths for his name's sake. Even though I walk through the darkest valley, I will fear no evil for you are with me; your rod and your staff, they comfort me.
>
> You prepare a table before me in the presence of my enemies. You anoint my head with oil; my cup overflows.
>
> Surely your goodness and love will follow me all the days of my life, and I will dwell in the house of the LORD forever. [Ps. 23:1–6 NIV]

> Love, Your proud and admiring brother.

New Avenues of Ministry

Retirement has been a comma in my life, definitely not a full stop. Since completing paid employment, I have enjoyed a slower pace from the frenetic activity and decision-making opportunities of an aged care facility. On my first day of not working, I revelled in the warmth of the sun in my garden, contemplated red geraniums, and indulged in reading. There were no deadlines, no emails, no people, and no time sheets to sign.

Since that first day of freedom, I have holidayed. I have supported an eight-year-old girl with her reading, concentration, and maths skills. I have enjoyed volunteer pastoral care, visiting in the renal units of the local hospitals. Another pleasure has been teaching English to a diligent Chinese mum. There have been opportunities for conducting the occasional church service, and for focusing on writing. I signed up to be a health volunteer with the Department of Physiotherapy at Macquarie University. This means that I offer myself for interviews with their doctoral students.

My employers graciously allowed me to purchase the house that I have been living in for the past twelve years as part of my employment arrangement. The house settlement is an occasion of great joy after much saving, investing, and receiving of gifts. It provides a sense of continuity and stability made possible, in part, by the generosity of family and friends.

14

God Gives Breath

for the Marathon

HAVING DESCRIBED SOME of the significant events of my outer life, I want to now suggest ways which I have found helpful to develop mental and spiritual energy for nurturing my inner life.

I sometimes liken my body and its impairments to a putt-putt car engine that dreams to have the "zhooom-zhooom" of a V-8 machine. This vision may not be particularly realistic, at least physically. But any engine, whether it rattles on slowly or revs with supercharged force, needs fuel to keep it going. Those of us who have cerebral palsy know that fatigue, brought on by the immense effort it takes to move, is a common symptom. We need high-quality energy sources to sustain our dreams.

The next section of this book relates to the high-octane fuel I need to flood my mind and spirit so that at least they can thrive on a V-8 capacity. Catalysts are vital to energise what I hope to be a life of loving service as a Christ-follower. To use another metaphor which underlies this book: an athlete, whether elite or one like me, who pads along the stadium to the best of her ability, needs breath to bring oxygen to the muscles and blood. I believe God breathes life into us, energising us to take the next step.

I will focus on healing, aspects of Christian spirituality, a sense of belonging to Christian community, and the human experiences of romance, love, family, films, and music. Each of these dimensions gives me "umph". Bear with me as I touch on these speckled facets of colour which bring me hope. Through these different lenses, I see God at work. God is at the same time barracking for me on the sidelines and infusing breath into my being.

What Is Life-Giving in Thinking about Healing?

When things go awry in our experience, there is sometimes a nagging sense that we are being punished. A person with a disability, when comparing their health with the health of others, may have a niggling sense of guilt about their very existence. I admit that when several strings of challenging events happen to me in quick succession, I am tempted to ask, "What am I doing wrong?"

However, the words of Jesus, in the context of the healing of a blind man, are a kind corrective to this skewed thinking. "Neither this man sinned nor his parents sinned" (John 9:1–2 NIV). This insight paves the way from a sense of guilt to grace. Punishment has nothing to do with the experience of disability. My understanding is that God looks at us with the eyes of love. God's heart is especially in tune with those who suffer and struggle.

Be that as it may, the issue of healing is fraught with questions, some of which I have wrestled with personally. For example, why are some healed from sickness and others not? Why are some people born with disability and some are not?

If you are looking for easy answers, then I will disappoint. However, I share what I know to be true for myself. For the moment, I am content to live with unanswered questions, although I have jokingly said to friends, "When my time comes, I'll be first in the queue to ask God about the curly conundrums that occupy thinking people's minds on earth!" Whether my questions are answered or not, I believe that I need to have at least wrestled with what a life-giving view of healing might be.

Some well-meaning people have said to me, as they look at my physical disability, "If you had more faith, you would be healed." I find that statement difficult, hurtful, and, I believe, not the complete truth. I have known many who are faith-filled and who walk closely with God, and yet who suffer with severe disability. In fact, I agree with another statement: "It takes more faith to live as a person with a disability in a wheelchair than it does to be healed."[1] Living with lifelong disability for me, requires a combination of tenacity and a reliance on God for daily strength. God's strength is made perfect in my weakness, as 2 Corinthians 12:9 reminds me. When I admit my neediness, God is responsive and runs to my side.

Having said that, I am sympathetic to the aims of the Christian ministry of healing which actively prays for health and wellness. While on earth, Jesus was continually working towards people's health, with compassion for those who struggled. We, too, can do no other if we are to follow in his footsteps.

Here are two examples.

- My first encounter with the healing ministry happened when I was a teenager. Dad took me to a church where a faith healer was visiting. My father was a level-headed man, not prone to fits of excitement, so the occasion was low-key and I was not aware of any artificial hype. He walked me slowly, without my sticks, up to the front of the sanctuary, holding me by my waist from behind as he sometimes did. There we met with an unassuming, balding, older man who took my hands. My dad still held me firmly. The healer began to pray earnestly, grunting, gasping, and groaning as he did so. Suddenly a power like cannon balls surged through my two bent legs. This was a definite strengthening physical sensation, unlike any I had experienced before or since. This unusual, pleasant feeling was repeated two or three times. We then returned to our seats.

I was not physically healed. However, I was not disappointed, but rather quietly content. We were tiptoeing on the edge of mystery. I felt affirmed and loved by God. The divine words I sensed in my spirit whispered, "You won't be healed physically, Heather, but this uplifting experience is to show you that I love you deeply, no matter what, and I will never forget you."

• Another experience of the healing ministry occurred while I attended Castle Hill Church.

The minister at the time asked me, "Heather, would you be interested in taking a turn conducting a healing service at the Kentgrove Church?" At first, I was struck by the irony of the situation—a wheelie leading prayers and reflections for healing. I chuckled to myself. What an incongruous picture. Eventually I said yes, understanding a little of what it means to be a wounded healer. Jesus himself, as crucified, could be described as such. From the place of pain, he offered words of hope and comfort to those around him. Could I not, as his follower, be an agent of healing too? The psychoanalyst C. G. Jung underlined the truth of this possibility by saying, "Only the wounded physician heals."[2]

Many books have been written on the subject of healing. I cannot do justice here to the depth of discussion needed. Instead, I offer a few introductory thoughts.

God has given the human body a wonderful capacity to heal itself, in many instances without medical intervention. When medical intervention is required, I believe that medication, skilled doctors, counsellors, and other health professionals can be agents of God in the healing process, whether this happens instantaneously or over time.

Healing is just as important for emotional wounds as it is for the physical dimension. Psychological wellness can have a positive effect on the physical health of the body. Conversely, resentment and holding grudges can play their part in eating away at a body's strength. Physical and emotional health are closely entwined. I have heard it preached at some healing services that we can be healed from the inside out.

While we must continue to pray and work towards health, there comes a point when we need to surrender to God's bigger picture, trusting him for the outcome. We cannot demand that God answer our prayers in one way only. We have to look at the words of Jesus in the midst of crucifixion for the ultimate cry of faith: "Father, into your hands, I commit my spirit" (Luke 23:46 NIV).

In fact, in the bigger scheme of things, people with disability and others who suffer have a part to play, just as they are, in igniting the light of faith in others. Richard Rohr, a Franciscan priest, develops this thought further:

> Julian of Norwich, my favourite English mystic said proudly: "Our wounds are our very trophies!" They are the "holes in the soul" where the Light and the Life can break through. Exactly as Leonard Cohen's Anthem puts it: "Forget your perfect offering / There is a crack in everything / That's how the light gets in."[3]

Finally, I am called to be available and faithful to God, whether I am physically able or not. God has given me gifts. Jesus's Parable of the Talents urges that I am accountable for how I use them (Matt. 25:14–30).

Drinking from the Wells of Christian Spirituality

The richness of my Christian faith tradition gives me breath for the marathon. What follows are selected qualities which are vital in nourishing me.

Honest Faith

Because I have had lifelong experience of disability, parts of which have been tough, I have been particularly attracted to the biblical accounts which realistically portray the rugged side of human existence. The Christian faith and its strong Jewish roots provide avenues for joyful strength and thankfulness to a God who provides for his children.

The tradition also validates expressing honesty, grief, and a sense of being forsaken. I particularly resonate with the Jewish psalms of lament, which certainly do not condone an easy, frothy triumphalism. Rather than point me in the direction of deeper depression, reading these psalms assures me that I am not alone in my down times. So-called heroes of the faith are naked before the living God. There is no pretence. They call it like it is, good and bad. Over many generations, faith-filled people show their solidarity with the rest of groaning humanity. Have a look at some of the Psalms and breathe in their authenticity and be encouraged (see especially Psalms 22, 6, 13, 38, 55, 77).

On the other side of the coin, we are called to be thankful, bringing to mind God's blessings. Psalms 8, 100, 103, 105, and 150 are some of many psalms which celebrate God's generosity. The simple joys of relaxing in another's company, soaking in the brilliant colours of creation, and savouring the gift of pleasant memories are all springboards for gratefulness to the divine One. Gratitude opens up the lungs for breath to flow through.

In the New Testament too, I find comfort in the life of Jesus Christ. The crucifixion and the resurrection are equally valid experiences. When I look at the crucifixion of the earthly Jesus, I sense a strong connection between him and me. He shares in my suffering and I in his. In a strange way, my physical paralysis is intertwined with his. At the moment of crucifixion, he is pinned. He cannot escape. He cannot move. He is in excruciating pain. In this way, he chooses to identify strongly with me and other disempowered ones.

Despair is not the end of the story, though. Resurrection, both for Christ and his wounded followers, is a sign of a reinvigorated life. With every wound, there is the possibility of hope and another beginning. Whenever a person refuses to be confined by their limitations, they are reflecting again a new energy in the resurrected Christ himself.

Prayer: A Lifeline

There are many kinds of prayer, some of which I explore later in the "Nurturing your Spirit" section (appendix H). However, for me, "arrow" prayers are a vital means for regulating breath for my life marathon. These short, sharp, often urgent requests, as part of an ongoing prayerful relationship, are heartfelt. Precarious transfers from one seat to another, for example, when it looks likely I will tumble to the floor, are occasions in point. God is particularly responsive to neediness. An exquisite late discovery of a prayer from the Psalms hits the spot for me. "Hear my cry, O God; listen to my prayer. From the ends of the earth I call to you, I call as my heart grows faint. Lead me to the rock that is higher than I." (Psalm 61:1-2 NIV)

A prayer of availability, on the other hand, requires commitment on my part at any time, but is appropriately uttered at the beginning of the day. It goes something like this: "Hey, God, this is a new day. I wonder what you have in mind for its minutes and hours. When you want me to play a part in sharing your compassion with someone, give me a nudge. I am available."

I find prayer can also be a great change agent for a lousy attitude, especially when I think I am becoming too precious. Meister Eckhart, the German mystic, talks about the importance of sensing and soaking in the presence of God and its effect on our relationship with others. He states, "What a [person] takes in by contemplation, that he [or she] pours out in love."[4]

Humility

Humility is a value I prize in my Christian journey. It is not a grovelling spirit which diminishes the wonder of our very selves. Rather, it is closely connected with a teachable attitude.

When I first started tertiary education, I thought I would learn so much. Knowledge can be powerful and can open doors which would otherwise remain firmly shut. However, the more I learned, the more I realised I did not know. So-called answers lead invariably to a thousand more questions. Instead of education providing solutions, it often teaches us to ask more, thereby delving into deeper mystery. Humility is an attitude that many scholars develop as they stand on the edge of the unknown. If humility is a desirable quality in the academic field, then it is equally important to nurture it in our spirit lives.

There are three quotations which I believe capture humility as a vital quality in my Christian pilgrimage.

F. B. Meyer, a Christian thinker, states: "I used to think, that God's gifts were on shelves—one above another, and the taller we grow, the easier we can reach them. Now I find that God's gifts are on shelves—one beneath another, and the lower we stoop, the more we get!"[5]

C. S. Lewis, another Christian scholar who did not bask in intellectual superiority, reminds us, "Don't shine so that others can see you. Shine so that through you, others may see Him (God)."[6]

Hafiz, a Persian poet living in the fourteenth century, humbly asserts, "I am a hole in a flute that the Christ's breath moves through."[7]

This last piece of wisdom profoundly uncovers the insight that the divine One is our life source. There is no room for the delusion that we are self-sufficient. This can be freeing in the sense that I am not totally responsible for all that happens. Rather, God and I are partners in bringing to life his mission.

We Depend on Each Other

Western society prizes the quality of independence in so-called successful people. Independence has its place in certain situations, but exercised in its extreme, it robs us of the blessing of community and inter-dependence. You only have to look at 1 Corinthians 12 to realise that Christians as the body of Christ on earth are closely connected and need each other to faithfully live out their vocations. Energy and effectiveness are increased when we work together.

> There are different kinds of gifts, but the same Spirit distributes them. There are different kinds of service, but the same Lord. There are different kinds of working, but in all of them and in everyone it is the same God at work.
>
> Now to each one the manifestation of the Spirit is given for the common good. To one there is given through the Spirit a message of wisdom, to another

> a message of knowledge by means of the same Spirit,
> to another faith by the same Spirit, to another gifts
> of healing by that one Spirit, to another miraculous
> powers, to another prophecy, to another distinguishing
> between spirits, to another speaking in different kinds
> of tongues, and to still another the interpretation of
> tongues. All these are the work of one and the same
> Spirit, and he distributes them to each one, just as he
> determines. (1 Cor. 12:4–11 NIV)

Moses, an Old Testament leader, knew the value of his offsiders as they supported him during Israel's battle against the Amalekites.

> So Joshua fought the Amalekites as Moses had ordered,
> and Moses, Aaron and Hur went to the top of the
> hill. As long as Moses held up his hands, the Israelites
> were winning, but whenever he lowered his hands,
> the Amalekites were winning. When Moses' hands
> grew tired, they took a stone and put it under him
> and he sat on it. Aaron and Hur held his hands up—
> one on one side, one on the other—so that his hands
> remained steady till sunset. (Exod. 17:10–12 NIV)

People with disability bear witness in our very existence to the biblical principle of relying on each other in times of need. We challenge the myth of self-sufficiency. Even corporate leaders need others around them. In an annual report, an executive director of a big company is alleged to have said, "My staff do not support me. They carry me."[8]

Belonging to a Christian Community

Building on this idea of dependence on each other, I suggest that belonging to a Christian community is vital breath in my pilgrimage as a person with disability. One of my faith-filled carers reminded me once, "You don't have many nearby family or children of your own, but don't forget you have lots of brothers and sisters in your church. It's a big responsibility." She underlined the importance of my spiritual family, who encourage me and with whom, in turn, I hope to share faith.

Church has its foibles like any group, but it still aims to be the face, hands, and feet of Christ in a hurting world. Many hospitals and other welfare agencies have their origin in the Christian community. Yet there are some people who say to me, "I can worship God just as well on the golf course as I can in church." That might be true, but solitary Christianity misses out on the communal blessing which God has given us to inspire us to greater heights. Being in a community can also challenge our prejudices and is a corrective against the self-absorption of the "me" generation.

There have been times when the embers of my faith have burnt low. Doubts have occasionally assailed me. At these times, the experience of the loving support of the community of faith has helped me to find my way again. In one sense, I borrowed the faith of my fellow Christians to rediscover the first love of God in a deeper way. In fact, one of the most powerful ways I experience the divine is through the kindness of others.

My current faith community is Terrigal Uniting Church. This large worshipping and community centre comprises a number of different congregations, and has been my spiritual home for a long time now. Its diversity, both in age and theological expression, is remarkable. I like its Christian encouragement, its emphasis on strong lay and ordained leadership, its vital pastoral care network, and its welcoming care of people in joyful, ordinary, and crisis times. We financially support different fundraising community and church projects every year.

A big part of the church community's energy is channelled through community outreach. Individually and together, members are involved in chaplaincy ministries, education and teaching, hospitality, and other efforts. Generosity prevents staleness and isolationism.

We are stronger together than alone. (See appendix A for a discussion on how to encourage a welcoming church.)

Romance, Love, Friendship, and Family

A Christian community has given me the sense of belonging to a global network of caring, faithful people. Equally important to me is the affection I have given and received in my close personal relationships. These have given me cause to ponder, nourishing the garden of my heart over the years. A marathon run with God-given friends makes the effort easier. To use a sporting metaphor which I have discovered in my swimming sessions: if you can find yourself in another's slipstream, life can be a breeze!

My journey to find the slipstream in the area of romantic involvement has been marked with both joy and disappointment. In my teen years and my twenties, especially as my friends began to marry, I looked wistfully at bridal fashions in shop windows. I planned my possible wedding service and venues, even down to music and bridesmaids. It was just a minor technicality to find the groom!

It is true that I have received three proposals of marriage. One was from a dear ninety-three-year old man when I was thirty-something. Although I did not feel drawn to the prospect of those particular lifelong partnerships, I warmly appreciated their friendships.

One of my hard-won learning curves has been to accept graciously a closed door when a romantic relationship I wanted to blossom didn't. I have invisible yet real scars around my tender heart to prove it. I am blessed, though, that over time those yearnings have lessened in strength.

I have now come to realise that my vocation in life has been to experience the love of many, rather than the love of one. If marriage had come to fruition, then I would not have been able to devote my time and energy with the same vigour to the chaplaincy work about which I became so passionate. In my younger days, I was starry-eyed about romance, but life experience has grounded me.

In my personal and professional life, many have confided in me about their tumultuous marriages. While I realise that there are also many healthy relationships, I have learned that life-giving connections require hard work. I also observe that kind people of good will on both sides of a relationship do not always make compatible partners. Any one of us has the capacity to hurt another. Interests which begin as mutual can change over time. Adaptability and flexibility are not always in bountiful supply.

My desire to be a mum was never as great as my desire to be a wife. Observing pale, heavy-eyed friends raise babies and toddlers, to the point of depletion, was enough to warn me off that treadmill. Try as I might, I could not imagine changing nappies, bathing kids, and running to keep up with their lightning movements, given the disability I have. I would live in daily dread of unwittingly running babies over with my wheelchair and leaving tyre marks on their tummies!

However, there were two significant points when I grieved for the maternal life that could have been. Firstly, when I turned thirty, I realised the biological clock was ticking. Secondly, following a hysterectomy, I realised that any flickering hope of motherhood had finally been extinguished. For a day or two I was wistful, wandering around in a daze. I also realise that these feelings might have been compounded by post-operative blues. Emotional fragility is a painful part of recovery. If someone even looked at me the wrong way at that stage, I felt like the shards of a broken vase.

Despite these feelings, I get immense joy from nursing tiny babies belonging to mums who are brave enough to let me have a cuddle. To nurture the little ones who are vulnerable seems to call something mysterious and wonderful from deep inside of me. I sit sometimes in awe of tiny, curling fingers and little fingernails, raising a cheer for life in miniature.

Seeing my niece and nephews develop from babyhood gave me much pleasure. Newborn life is such an awe-inspiring miracle. I am realistic enough, though, to know that the nitty-gritty of everyday care of children is exhausting. For brief times, I burped and got sicked on with the best of them, but then again, I was able to hand the bundles of joy back.

Marriage and motherhood did not eventuate for me. But, importantly, I have discovered that I can channel my caring instincts into other avenues. Relationships, whether intimate or wide-ranging, are God's gift to me. They remind me that I do not run the marathon alone.

Music

Music as a form of artistic expression has the potential to inspire me greatly. Whether it is simply to provide a pleasant backdrop to a demanding exercise routine, or to transport me to other realms—spiritual and emotional—I do not underestimate music's power to give me life when my light is flickering.

My preferences tend to be on the light classical spectrum. "Jesu, Joy of Man's Desiring" by J. S. Bach, "Comfort ye my people" from Handel's *Messiah*, or "Pie Jesu" by Andrew Lloyd Webber encourage me to fly when my mind becomes flat or too confined. Music for me does not have to be only religious. Chopin and Mozart are composers who can soothe my troubled mind or stimulate the joy bubbling inside me.

I am showing my age when I say I love the groovy rhythms of Abba. Some brass band music can cause my toes to tap.

What has music to do with breath for the marathon? Simply, it adds zest to my life, accesses the right side of my brain, and communicates deeply with my spirit when words fail.

Films

Similarly, films which are inspirationally biographical, like *The King's Speech*—the story of King George VI's battle to overcome a stammer—can give me energy to keep going on my life's stadium circuit.

My Left Foot, the moving story of a growing boy with cerebral palsy which I alluded to earlier, enabled me to grieve more fully for the losses associated with my disability.

Awakenings is the wonderful story of a neurologist's attempts, via drug experimentation, to raise to life some of his patients who were in catatonic states. Because of his interventions, some were able to experience a summer of love and enjoyment. For me this movie was about seizing fleeting opportunities for sparkle and joie de vivre when they come.

Dances with Wolves was a sharp reminder to me to be culturally sensitive to the needs of minority groups like the Native Americans. A good film can enthuse, chasten, and ignite a flagging spirit.

Final Thoughts

We are now approaching the finish line of my inner reflections which give energy to my outer life. As I look back on the memories of my marathon journey so far, I reflect on times when it was hard to maintain momentum, on times when stones caught in my shoes, on times when my wheels punctured and slowed me down, and on times when I took mighty tumbles.

However, I am also thankful for the many spectators who cheer me on my way. I honour my fellow runners and wheelers who show me possibilities of how to run the race. I am grateful for the presence of the divine One who is both my barracker and breath.

In a strange way, my precarious start in life has led me to a sense of destiny. I firmly believe my life was graciously spared for God-given purposes. While I have difficulty believing that my life is strictly pre-destined, I do hold that life is sacred, and that I am accountable to the divine One for the choices I make with the precious gift given to me. Even my early welcome to the world, announced in an Australian Presbyterian newsletter, foreshadowed a life of possibility. At the time I was called the church's "littlest missionary."

Such a description speaks of a combination of vulnerability and strong purpose. God's wish for you and me is often realised in the face of so-called weakness and unpromising beginnings. In fact, some have assumed, especially when I was younger, "You have lived a shel-tered life." Looking back on my dash on earth so far, I can say I have lived to the beat of a different drum. It is a life of colour and shade. Some memories are delightfully happy, some harrowing, some mun-dane. To say that I have been supported wonderfully is true, but who could say I have always lived an easy, protected existence? Challenges have forced me to look to God for my strength when I have felt most weak. They have forced me to reflect and not rush through life.

What blessing is there to be enjoyed by plodding athletes like us in the slow lane? What is the arena of our mission, if you like? Some able-bodied people, having read this book, might be tempted to think that the events and possible achievements are ordinary. Compared to some in the able-bodied world, life with disability could be perceived as ho-hum, shaped by limitations.

Ultimately, though, our triumph is in the world of the spirit. It lies in our availability and responsiveness to the nudges of the Spirit, rather than viewing ourselves as victims of unkind fate. Along the way, impairment tests our ability to push our boundaries, developing qualities like perseverance. Our inner lives need to be nurtured regularly in order for us to live with and transcend the difficulties we face. For me personally, I am fed by prayer, Spirited companionship, and reading.

However, our journey should not be focused purely on self-development, important though that is. You and I have a responsibility to look beyond our interior battles to the fellow humans with whom we are inextricably connected. We have the opportunity to meet people who assist us in a variety of ways. Potentially, we have eyes to observe people and events which other, hurried humanity may not have time to notice as deeply. Along with the capacity to soak in our surroundings comes the responsibility to respond to need compassionately.

Further, I ponder that even if I did know the biological why of my disability, the answer to the question would not help me to live a faith-filled life. To express myself creatively in a Christ-honouring way means I want to pay special attention to those who might be wounded and excluded at some time in their lives. Let's face it. Have we not all been there?

Compassionate relationships with those who did not quite fit in were the very focus of Jesus's earthly ministry. He restored them to community. A gentle hope I have is to include those on the outside, rather than to exclude those I do not yet understand. There are some who say that the aim to include is superfluous because, at least in God's eyes, we are already together and one. Nevertheless, I long for the time when our actions enable God's dream for more understanding of each other to be realised. A marathon run (or wheeled) is not a solitary endeavour which prizes only lone achievement. Our winning is tied in with encouraging others to reach their potential as well.

In my courageous moments, I venture to say, "Bravo to those who are a bit different, because we challenge the status quo. We can become the catalyst for a positive change in personal attitude, a change in architecture, a change in a systemic flaw. I quote the French, "vive la différence!"

Despite this unique colour that people with disability bring, I sometimes reflect on how life could have been different without disability. I wonder about the track not travelled. But too many steps down this path of impossibility weaken my precious energy and focus. Even in these occasional detours into wistfulness, I am surrounded by countless kind-hearted people who urge me to keep on wheeling the marathon. By their words, attitudes, and example, they keep my torch burning. Good friends are indeed life-giving. A whacky sense of humour and authentic sharing of feelings are real blessings. I am thankful to those who have added sparkle to life in the arena.

Individually and with the support of others, I make the best of what I can do, rather than what I can't. God's universe and cosmic purposes are far bigger than my miniature world, but I still want to play my part in making a positive difference. To be available to God in shining a light means I want to be more flexible, less self-absorbed and other-focused. I am drawn to Bessie Anderson Stanley's definition of success. I like it because it is not wrapped up in the traditional indicators of wealth and power. She states, "To know that even one life has breathed easier because you have lived, this is to have succeeded."[9]

Although my arena of ministry is more focused now, God's compassion can flourish among the people with whom I touch base each day, whether they are care workers, shop assistants, taxi drivers, students, neighbours, health care professionals, or social media friends.

I believe too that often our influence is unintentional and unconscious. I am both encouraged and challenged by Jesus' parable of the last judgement in the gospel of Matthew. When Jesus exhorted his followers to feed the hungry, clothe the naked, and visit the prisoners, some of his listeners showed genuine surprise, saying, "When did we see you hungry and give you food, or thirsty and give you something to drink?" (Matthew 25:37 NIV) Imagine their look of puzzlement when they could not understand the power of their unexpected influence. Jesus shared some startling wisdom, declaring, "Whatever you did for one of the least of these brothers [or sisters] of mine, you did it for me" (Matthew 25:40 NIV) You never know who is watching in the spectator stands or on the field as others search for a helpful hint in the running of their particular race. It could be that our resilient purpose, shaped by the hands of God, will give a neighbour strength for the next step on his or her own Olympic journey.

Undergirding the sense of community spirit which I am encouraging is Someone even more sustaining. Who gives me the breath, the energy, the courage for my marathon? In strength and weakness, I am comforted and, yes, emboldened again by the words of Dietrich Bonhoeffer, one of my faith heroes, who reminds me to whom I belong.

Who am I? ...

Whoever I am, Thou knowest, O God, I am Thine![10]

APPENDICES: HINTS AND REFLECTIONS ON EVERYDAY LIVING FOR PEOPLE WITH DISABILITY

Introduction

FROM PERSONAL REFLECTIONS, we now move on to very practical considerations which can either help or hinder our daily journeys. It is unusual to have such a large proportion of a book devoted to appendices. However, I trust that this format will add to the simplicity and clarity of the down-to earth hints for people with disability and those who support and work with them. I hope that the pointers will not only relate to people with cerebral palsy but have a general appeal to those who have other forms of physical disability. The list structure with occasional illustrations will make it easier for interested people to cherry-pick items which are of most use to them.

APPENDIX A

A Welcoming Church Including People with Disability

I AM ENCOURAGED by the accounts in Jesus's life in which he spends much of his time with people with disability, such as the woman who is bent, and people with hearing and sight impairments. He takes special notice of those who struggle.

When John the Baptist is languishing in prison, he doubtfully asks Jesus, "Are you the one who is to come, or should we expect someone else?" (Matthew 11:3 NIV)

Jesus sends back encouragement to John. "The blind receive sight, the lame walk, those who have leprosy are cured, the deaf hear" (Matthew 11:5 NIV)

In other words, one of the marks of Jesus's messianic claim is the investment he makes in the lives of those with disability.

As Christ followers, the Christian community aims to capture the compassionate spirit of their Master in enabling people with disability to reach their potential. There is much the church can do to make the lives of people with all sorts of disabilities not only more comfortable, but enhanced in quality. As Christians we also need to find ways of discovering the giftedness in people with disability, so that their contribution is recognised.

Our mission with people with disability has a large scope, but, for the sake of this book, I will concentrate on those with mobility challenges.

- If your friend with a disability wishes, then having you sit down with them in the pew while the rest of the congregation stands to sing can be an act of solidarity.

- Make sure that their mobility aids are as close as possible to them in the pews.

- Physical access, such as accessible parking, ramps, purpose-built toilets, and flat non-slip surfaces must be provided. Carpets rather than rugs are a safer option. Those of us who preach or take leadership roles in the church appreciate ramp access to the sanctuary.

- Be alert for wet, slippery surfaces for those on walking sticks and frames. Wipe up spills immediately. Safety for people with disability is good safety practice for everyone.

- Cushions for hard pews may be more comfortable.

- Ensure that a person in a wheelchair is positioned so they can have visual access to the worship leaders and any viewing screen. Sometimes wheelies unintentionally get a great bird's-eye view of people's backsides as they stand to sing hymns.

- While it is important to allow space to ensure safe passage of processions, it is equally important not to place people in wheelchairs out of the way, emphasising their ostracism from the rest of the Christian community. The advantage of flexible seating is that it is possible to remove a single chair to enable a person in a wheelchair to be flush with the rest of the congregation, not sticking out into the aisle.

  To illustrate: Church pews were repositioned without fuss before three family weddings, so that I could still be part of the congregation and not impede exuberant bridal parties walking down the aisle.

- Ensure that wheelies and others with mobility impairments are provided with support at refreshment gatherings.

- If it is within your capacity, and safe to do so, it may be helpful to offer transport to people who are challenged in getting out and about.

- If travel by car is difficult, consider the possibility of the church subsidising the cost of an accessible taxi fare occasionally.

- In your planning, make sure that most of your church activities are disability-inclusive. Consider the access, type of event, transport options, and people support available.

- Churches have different traditions regarding the conduct of Communion. Some congregations go forward to the sanctuary to receive the bread and wine; others are served in the pews. Negotiation as to what would be comfortable for the person with a disability is vital. Some churches have a designated server who roams the congregation to assist those who find it difficult to process to the front.

- It is tempting to think that once access issues are addressed, all the boxes are ticked in disability ministry. That is only the beginning. Make sure that the ministry of the whole person is operating. Take time to listen to stories and identify needs. Be creative in meeting them where possible. Ministry with people is not limited to worship on Sundays (or whenever your religious observance is held).

- On occasion, let your prayers, sermons, and homilies address the specific concerns of people with disability. Frustration at physical limitation, pain management, patience in waiting for people, medical appointments, potential isolation at home, exclusion, medical research facilities, disability group homes, and creativity for disability policymakers are all topics which provide good material for reflection.

- Ensure that your theology—that is, your view of God and your understanding of the gospel—is life-giving. For example, prosperity doctrine, which emphasises God's blessing only on the rich and the successful, is woefully inadequate for those who struggle in life and live on limited incomes. Triumphalism, which suggests that all you need to do is to have faith and everything will turn out OK, is damaging and untrue. The wonderful truth of the gospel is that the crucifixion and the resurrection are both valid, sometimes coexisting experiences for the Christ-follower.

If you wish to see a wonderful exploration of the theology of people with disability and their vital presence, both in church and in the community, I recommend an article by J. E. Lesslie Newbigin, a British writer and bishop who worked in the Church of South India. It suffices at this stage to mention one piece of his wisdom, which is clothed in the language of his time:

> The poor, deprived, the handicapped are not primarily a problem to be solved by the rich, the

comfortable and the strong. They are bearers of a witness without which the strong are lost in their illusions. They are trustees of a blessing without which the Church cannot bless the world. Their presence in the Church is the indispensable corrective of our inveterate tendency to identify the power of God with our power, the victory of God with our success. It is the illusion of the strong, the healthy to see themselves in the centre and the handicapped as those on the margins. The Church should be freed from the illusion by the presence in the centre of its life of the cross of him who suffered there.[1]

- An occasional service on the theme of the positive contribution of people with disability may heighten awareness in this area.

- Without paralysing people's spontaneity in an effort to be politically correct, it is still helpful to concentrate on using words and language that empower people with disability rather than demean them. For example, the term "people with disability" is much to be preferred to "cripple" or "invalid." The words "ministry with" are less patronising than "ministry to."

- Where at all possible, people with disability should be encouraged to physically join in worship, community, and service. However, limitations make that difficult. Make sure your ministry expands to pastoral visiting, phone calls, and prayer with those who are confined to home or a care facility.

- Technology can be used to advantage, assuming the members of your congregation with mobility impairments are comfortable with operating a computer. Recording sermons on your website and updating your website and social media pages are other ways to include people who may be geographically isolated. Yet another form of ministry may involve texting messages of encouragement on mobile phones.

- If the person with mobility impairments is gifted, has potential, and is willing, encourage them to participate in the leadership of worship, including prayers, readings and talks. They may also enjoy participating in the welcoming or hospitality team, crèche duty, administration, IT maintenance, writing, pastoral care by phone, and so on. My observation of many churches is that only a few people assume responsibility for the majority of the tasks to be completed, leaving some to be overburdened and ragged around the edges. Would it not be preferable if work could be shared more equally among those whose gift it is, including people with disability? This welcome to ministry may require a little creativity to enable strengths to be optimised and weaknesses minimised, but hey, it is worth the effort.

To sum up, the church as the body of Christ is not complete without the presence and contribution of people with disability.

The apostle Paul exhorts the early Corinthian Christians to pay special honour to those who are the weaker members of the body (1 Cor. 12:22-23). Open your heart and mind to the probability that you may receive ministry from those who live a little differently to you. God's presence may come to you in unusual disguises.

APPENDIX B

Surviving the Difficulties and Frustrations of Living with Disability

I would now like to lay out hints on how to survive and, yes, even thrive (hopefully with a touch of style) in a life with physical difference. Friends and families get a look-in too, as I offer my two pennies' worth of thinking about how able-bodied people and people with disability can work as a team to bring each other energy on the road we all travel.

Most days I can cope, after a fashion, with the challenges of living with disability. On some days I can be creative when obstacles arise. Most days I can manage with graciousness and tolerance. But on other days, the devil on my left shoulder roars more loudly than the angel on my right, especially when I am sleep deprived.

The following hints may possibly deepen the insight of the poor, unsuspecting bystanders who sometimes have to absorb the ire of their struggling friends with disability. More often than not, the anger we express is more to do with our own frustrations than your perceived ineptitude. Please, be patient with us as we wrestle with our internal demons. Occasionally we rise above the battle. Occasionally we lose.

We, like you, need the mercy of God and the understanding of friends to bind our wounds.

Attitudes

- Condescension and the making of assumptions about people's abilities are difficult for me to process. I find patronising actions and words demeaning when my own graciousness is in short supply. A light touch on the shoulder can be encouraging for some, but a pat on the head is a definite no-no. Assume people with disability are intelligent until conversation proves otherwise. Even if people do have intellectual impairment, they still deserve dignity and respect.

- When a person with a disability has to rely so much on the efforts of carers or family members for the supply of everyday needs, it is often difficult to express anger to those closest to them. There is a fear, whether legitimate or not, of payback.

Access

So-called accessible toilets which are not wheelchair-friendly heighten my blood pressure. Some have stairs to gain entry (yes, I have actually seen it!), heavy doors, second airlock doors, high mirrors, far too small circulation spaces for wheelchairs, inadequate back support on the cistern, wrongly placed or inappropriately angled rails, and difficult-to-reach flush buttons. Not having adequate facilities available severely limits your recreational or work options.

- High reception counters without provision for lower access puts a strain on the neck and can be isolating.

- Lack of accessible toilets on planes can limit opportunities for travel.

- Ineligible people pinching accessible parking spots can lead to inconvenience. This sometimes means that wheelies and others expend more energy to cover longer distances—occasionally in drenching rain.

Positive attitudes towards people with disability are vital in promoting healthy connections. However, they are not the complete story. Lack of town planning, political will, or finance to make neighbourhoods more physically accessible is demoralising. Decisions not to make vital modifications have great implications for a person's social life and emotional well-being. Physical barriers can lead to isolation at worst, lack of variety in work and recreational options at the very least. There are times when I wish I could swap places with politicians, town planners, and accountants so they could experience first-hand the physical barriers we face daily.

Communication

- Strangers taking liberties with terms of endearment, calling me "love," darling," or "sweetie" can make me uncomfortable. I appreciate that there is no hurt intended. I realise this approach might be helpful if you have forgotten their name, but these forms of address can be perceived as patronising. Personally, my family can get away with it, and I would make allowances for a tall, dark, handsome stranger inviting me on a smashing date. But otherwise, best not. There is something precious about hearing the sound of your preferred name, which bestows dignity.

- Lack of communication by community service providers, if service provision changes, keeps people out of the loop. Informing clients of progress or otherwise in their requests is courteous customer service. Silence can be demoralising. When there is a vacuum of information flow, speculation runs rife.

- People not listening or following through carefully on instructions for helping me leads to extra work for me or others. Alternatively, unexpected topples can occur. Ongoing communication between enabler and client or friend is vital.

Everyday Living

- The enormous effort it takes for everyday tasks can be slow and tiring. It can be surprising how much energy personal hygiene routines require.

- Always needing to plan to do simple things can be challenging. People with disability depend on the availability of carers or friends to help, suitability of access, right kind of transport, right kind of wheelchair for the activity, and help arrangement at the other end of the journey. Oh, for the spontaneous life! At least it sharpens our organisational skill.

- Dropping things on the floor with monotonous regularity can be irritating. The Coombes Law of Magnetism states: "The more tired you are, the greater the gravitational force of the earth, and the more items have a fascination for crashing to the floor." My long-handled, clawed picker-up tool is my trusty companion, even with small objects like tablets and coins.

- Christmas shopping or retail therapy at other peak times can be stressful. People in a rush can often step right in front of you quickly, without any indication, leaving you jittery because you are trying to avoid doing injury to their calves or ankles with your footplates. Children also have an undeveloped sense of space and can move quite unpredictably across your path.

- Sleeping upright in my wheelchair is exhausting. This happens when my motorised bed breaks down and is too high for my body to negotiate. At least I get to see late-night TV reruns of crime shows!

Community Support in Difficulty

- Gather teams of people around you for different levels of support, such as ambulance officers, fire and rescue workers, police, neighbours, taxi drivers, gardeners, and daily carers. Networking with a number willing support people can save putting a load on any one particular person.

  To illustrate: The electrical controller on my motorised wheelchair chose to give up the ghost when I was on my way to bed at 10:30 p.m. I could not move, even to my spare motorised vehicle at the other end of the house.

  I always carry my mobile phone around my neck. I rang the local fire brigade and told them of my predicament. Ten minutes later they arrived, with the help of an INS security box at my front door which enabled them to gain entry. One of the fire officers happened to be the father of a boy with muscular dystrophy. Consequently, he was an expert on motorised wheelchairs. He, along with his mates, moved the spare chair and assisted me with my transfer. God bless their cotton socks, their grins, and their big, burly muscles.

I rang the police once at night because I had wedged my wheelchair in between a stove and a cupboard. Don't ask me how. I couldn't move. They came round to the back of the house to find an open entrance. While waiting for them, I heard in the distance a muffled screech, followed by peals of laughter.

I found out later that one of the boys in blue had waded into a spider-laden cobweb in the dark. It spooked him, causing great hilarity among his colleagues. Knowing that gave me a warm feeling. Our wonderful constabulary are human too.

I have fondness also for ambulance officers. At particularly challenging times, they have eased me out of scrapes, especially when osteoarthritis arrived as an unwelcome intruder into my life. They have pulled me from the floor after I have fallen.

During one trip to hospital in an ambulance, an ambo with a wicked sense of humour sensed my anxiety and started to recite the twelve tribes of Israel. This diversionary tactic was totally surreal, but it calmed me down, made me giggle, and gave me courage to face the next challenge.

- Lobby politicians, councillors, and service providers for what you perceive your needs to be.

To illustrate: Australia is in the process of implementing a much-needed social reform which will benefit people with disability in the funding and delivery of care services. The National Disability Insurance Scheme did not appear overnight, but steadily blossomed, partly due to the lobbying of consumers with disability and other dedicated enthusiasts. *Every Australian Counts* is the e-newsletter which helped galvanise grass-roots support for this important milestone: *www.everyaustraliancounts.com.au*

a. We were encouraged to share our personal stories of disability experience, our financial challenges, and our accommodation preferences. Combined, this groundswell harnessed a sense of good will and political strength to finally realise the dream of consumer-directed service delivery.

b.   I live in an urban coastal area of New South Wales. My neighbourhood is a high-traffic area with dodgy, inaccessible footpaths which prevent my access to local shops and bus stops. I approached my local council to see if we could improve the situation. To their credit, they sent out a representative to hear my concerns. Because of alleged engineering difficulties and budgetary constraints, my approach was not ultimately successful, but at least I made a stand. You win some, you lose some. I will lobby again at another time.

c.   During a car trip, my then-eighty-year-old mother retrieved my wheelchair from the boot of the car so that I could enjoy a comfort stop. Upon arrival at the accessible facility, we discovered it was locked. A notice indicated the key was available at a community centre up the hill. Mum climbed the hill, asked for the key, and discovered it was mislaid. She walked down the hill and wheeled me back to the car. I puffed my way through another transfer. Mum lifted the chair into the boot. We drove to the next town, half an hour away, with me on an uncomfortably full bladder. The bliss of a fully equipped rest room! Not content to dismiss the issue, Mum and I wrote separate letters of concern to the council. They replied with admirable empathy and resolved to change their access procedure. There is an old proverb: "The squeakiest door gets the most attention."

•   Be a good neighbour to those who live geographically close to you whenever the opportunity presents itself. When crisis comes, those relationships can be mutually supportive.

To illustrate: Insistent rain pounded as the taxi drove me home. Rivers of water streamed down the windscreen as the wipers struggled to keep up. I was glad the driver was driving and not me. I trusted that he would navigate safely through the blurry ribbons of red and yellow tail- and headlights. I had heard news that very heavy rain was settling in for the next few days. It did not prepare me for the deluge of category 2 winds which howled upon my arrival home. Plants toppled, gates broke, power poles sparked. Trees staggered against the wrestling of the gales. Power was cut. House and street lights blackened. Landline phones fell silent.

Normally, I do not mind living alone, but reality began to rear its ugly head. My electric bed did not elevate or lower to assist me into and out of my sleeping place. I eyed my mobile phone carefully as the charge slowly disappeared. Not only is the phone one of my social outlets, it is a lifeline in an emergency. As moments ticked by, my power chair charge indicator urged me to conserve energy. I reduced my movement around my home, putting the chair on the slowest speed. Six thirty in the evening was enveloped with the blackness of midnight.

In the midst of this unfolding drama, my community care coordinator promised an evening care worker to assist me in the dilemmas. My neighbours (angels with shiny halos) promised to buy a battery-operated light for me. My worries for the safety of the evening carer driving in the horrific conditions were doubled when she failed to arrive. I later discovered that a fallen tree had blocked her drive.

There was still the challenge of how to get to bed. To the rescue came my neighbour, her husband, and her son, who lifted me into the bed. Necessity takes priority over pride and embarrassment. "Whatever works" is a philosophy to which I often subscribe. The angels arrived again next morning to see if I was OK to get out of bed.

Meanwhile, I believe that the advocacy of my community care coordinators prioritised resumption of electricity services in our area.

Friends popped in later in the day to reinforce that community spirit was alive and well. Neighbours arrived armed with a generator, which they connected up to my bed, wheelchair, and mobile phone.

I was overwhelmed by the kind initiative shown throughout this difficult experience, including from those who were undergoing their own storm challenges. People of good will can band together in adversity.

How does one conclude an appendix on frustration? Do we always need to find a positive? It is sometimes true that frustration can release energy to find a better solution. Sometimes it can make us stronger. Other times it just makes us mad. Sometimes we discover who our friends are when the chips are down.

The only options in these scenarios are to strengthen your links with community networks, let off steam with a friend (divine or human), have a chocolate, curl up with a good movie, punch a pillow, and go to bed early, ready to face a new day tomorrow!

APPENDIX C

Holidays Enrich Life for People with Disability

Holidays can certainly brush the cobwebs away and provide more zest for living. They can expand horizons and offer fresh perspectives. However, challenges in arranging disability-friendly holidays certainly test planning ability and sheer determination. Finding a travel companion experienced with my particular needs as a person with a disability is the first step. Locating wheelchair accessible accommodation is another. The lack of standardisation in symbols for wheelchair access in holiday directories is an anomaly. A symbol in a directory is no foolproof guarantee of wheelchair access.

Cruising has the advantage of being more restful. Continual packing and unpacking each day is not required. This mode of transport provides good value for money.

Air travel requires making sure to update oneself on each airline's policy on travellers with disability. If one cannot move independently to the airline seat, one can use a narrow, specially designed aircraft wheelchair to move within the aircraft. In Australia at least, the major airports normally have air bridges to facilitate access to the aircraft. Minor airports usually require the use of disabled person's lifters (DPLs or forklifts) to elevate and lower people who cannot negotiate the steps to and from the aircraft door. DPLs are weather dependent. On a couple of occasions I have had to postpone flights because it has been too windy or rainy to use one. Despite these inconveniences, airline staff members are normally very helpful.

In my later years, coach travel has become impossible because of high steps, but if you know where to look, there are wheelchair-accessible coach trips available.

There are some specialist travel agencies who concentrate on designing packages for people with disability. The Internet has been a godsend to facilitate the search for information.

Holidays for travellers with disabilities, believe it or not, can be stressful occasions, calling on flexibility and adaptability to cope with different routines, environments, and architecture which may not always be ideal.

Despite these ever-present hurdles, I was blessed to be more physically agile in my younger years, which enabled me to travel widely. Spreading my wings was made possible also because friends, free of marriage and family responsibilities, were available to accompany me.

Whether to the exotic destinations of my early years or the less ambitious locales of my older age, travel is a marvellous eye-opener to lives, cultures, and environments that are different from what I find in my backyard. What follows is only a selection of the adventures I have taken with friends or family.

Cairns, Queensland

A highlight of this car trip was a ferry ride to the beautiful, tropical Green Island. While on this glass-bottomed boat, I was fascinated by the coral of the Great Barrier Reef. I also eyed giant clams which were born three hundred years ago.

Dad carried me down several steps to see the beauty and diversity of a big underground aquarium. His dedication to me to ensure that I could participate as fully as possible was very moving.

Fiji

When I turned eighteen, one of my teachers from Spastic Centre Hostel days invited me for a holiday in Fiji, where she then lived. Imagine the novelty for me of bargaining with store owners in Suva over the going price of bags and brightly coloured clothes. Engaging with the multicultural interactions between Indians and Fijians was fascinating.

New Zealand

I thoroughly enjoyed the fun-loving companionship of five of our youth group members as we drove across the two islands of New Zealand. Apart from being enthralled by jet-boat rides, snow-capped mountains, geysers, and pristine lake scenery, other memories loom large. My friends hoisted me from my wheelchair to lie on the empty port-a-rack on top of our station wagon in an isolated part of the country. I was driven slowly for about a hundred yards while I surveyed the scene from my high vantage point, laughing.

Imagine another scene when our entourage were walking down the streets of windy Wellington. My faithful wheelchair pusher had broken his arm, and it was in a sling. That did not stop him from propelling my wheelchair one-armed. I had two huge bags of dirty washing on my tray as we wended toward the nearest laundromat. The sight of bedraggled young tourists evoked amusement in passing motorists, who beeped their horns in solidarity. We waved and smiled back.

I travelled in later years to the same beautiful country with my folks. Who could forget the entrancing highlight of hiring a helicopter and flying across the breathtaking Fox Glacier—such a big slice of God's wonderful creation? I saw the shadow of our flying craft etched on the ice, and I realised how small we were compared to the immense, stark beauty unfolded before us.

United Kingdom

Green fields, majestic castles, and exploring the roots of my British and Scottish ancestry were fabulous as I travelled by coach through England, Scotland, and Wales with my mum and dad. I "married" the coach driver in a mock wedding in Gretna Green. My dad, bedecked in a top hat and holding a pretend shotgun, stood by my side.

Who could forget three bemused Aussie tourists standing on the kerbside of chaotic Buckingham Palace Road, wondering how we were going to get across? Along stepped a well-dressed lady of aristocratic bearing. Seeing our dilemma, she confidently walked out on the road and held her right hand up in a stop signal. London traffic abruptly cowered to a standstill, and we sheepishly traversed the road, thankful for the unknown passer-by.

Such confidence among the British was shown again when we visited Windsor Castle to see the Horse Guard ceremony. My view was obstructed because I was seated at the back of a swirling crowd. We heard the bellowing voice before we saw the man rushing up behind us: "Make way for the invalid. Make way for the invalid," he boomed. The crowd parted like the Red Sea itself, and from then on we enjoyed a front-row vantage point.

Canada and the United States

The breathtaking alpine scenery of Canada, with its beautiful parks, squirrels, gardens, and glacial landscapes, captivated me. Mum accompanied me on a specialised disability tour, conducted in a wheelchair-accessible coach. Visiting Disneyland was entrancing. I enjoyed being a kid again, charmed by Cinderella and hugged by Goofy. My eyes were glued to singing puppets and fun-park rides in swirling cups and saucers. Universal Studies, Los Angeles, with its characteristic make-believe, was a magical glimpse into the world of film-making.

Photographer: Shirley Coombes

Norfolk Island

My abiding memory of this beautiful island holiday with two friends involved lying on a rug on grassland at night, looking across the expansive Pacific Ocean. When we looked upward, we gazed in wonder at millions and trillions of bright, twinkling stars, undimmed by artificial street light. This was a deeply spiritual experience.

> When I consider your heavens, the work of
> your fingers, the moon and the stars, which
> you have set in place, what is mankind that
> you are mindful of them, human beings
> that you care for them? (Ps. 8:3–4 NIV)

Clark Bay Farm, Narooma, South Coast, NSW

The tourist cabin on Clark Bay Farm, with its thoughtful, wheelchair-accessible features, gave me hope. The design included lifters, hoists, and spas, as well as easy-to-manoeuvre kitchen, bathroom, and bedrooms. Never before and never since have I experienced such a beautifully equipped resort. The usual effort associated with holidaying with disability was much less.

Tasmania Cruise

One of the many highlights of this idyllic, sunny cruise with Mum to Tasmania, an island off the mainland of Australia, was the kindness of a taxi driver who drove us around the environs of Burnie on shore leave. We visited gardens and feasted on blackberries by the side of the road. Scenic Mount Wellington and the Hobart Botanical Gardens, which we visited by wheelchair-accessible coach, are other special memories.

APPENDIX D

Humour Lubricates Awkward Situations

BORN THAT WAY by Eric Carlson is a book about a medical doctor with cerebral palsy of the athetosis type. He describes his experience of having to deliver an important speech in front of many dignitaries. When he was nervous, the wayward muscles in his arms and legs would shoot involuntarily and uncontrollably all over the place. He had to find a way of minimising the stress surrounding the important occasion. He decided he would remove his glasses during the speech, so that the only people he could clearly see were the ones in the immediate front row. The strategy worked.[1]

Humour also helped Mark Twain, the author, from getting out of a sticky situation while launching his lecturing career. During his maiden speech, Twain was trembling and perspiring in fear. He apparently said in his opening remarks: "Julius Caesar is dead. Shakespeare is dead. Napoleon is dead. Abraham Lincoln is dead, and I am far from well myself."[2]

Early on, I learned the value of humour to help myself and others feel at ease. Here are a few examples of how a sense of comedy lubricated otherwise tricky situations.

The Tale of the Persistent Emu

While meandering around in my manual wheelchair on the paths of a nearby Australian animal park with my family, I was suddenly aware of a mysterious presence creeping up behind me. It was not until "it" lurched to my right-hand side that I realised "it" was a big, waddling bird with a scrawny neck and long legs.

The emu holds pride of place in the Australian coat of arms, along with the kangaroo. There was nothing majestic about him that day, though. He was fascinated by the sparkle of the silver wheelchair rims twirling around. His neck straightened up after the close inspection. His small head and big beady eyes looked intently into mine, beginning a staring competition. I did not know who would break the gaze first. The encounter was reminiscent of a gun duel—a showdown at high noon at the OK Corral.

This national icon clearly had no idea of the subtleties of personal space. He was closer than close. I think my strangled scream scared him off ... at least for the moment. By this stage I did not know whether to be scared or amused. Suffice to say that I strongly encouraged my faithful wheelchair-pusher to hotfoot it to the nearest ladies' toilet.

With much panting, I tried to regain my composure by sitting on an available throne. My growing serenity was short-lived, however. Two big, brown eyes, a pointy beak, and a long neck peered around the toilet door. Can't a gal get a moment's peace? I exploded with laughter.

The Tale of the Ill-Timed Blackout

Conducting a wheelie friend's evening wedding rehearsal was a unique experience. The original plan was to rehearse outdoors, replicating the future choreography of the festive event. However, dark clouds, thunder, and lightning put paid to that idea.

We hastily relocated to the castle-like decor of a stately reception centre nearby. We went through the motions and the words of the ceremony so that each participant would feel comfortable with their parts the next day. A dramatic strike of lightning played havoc with the electricity supply as we were rehearsing the vows. We were plunged into darkness.

Not about to be defeated, one prepared friend offered a small torch to assist me, the celebrant, to read the appropriate responses. The atmosphere acquired an eerie quality as the faint light glowed on people's faces. Anyone who has viewed the TV show *The Addams Family*, whose characters live in a quirky mansion, might have a sense of the ambience.

Fortunately, the next day, the sun shone on the resplendent bride as she wheeled down the aisle to the musical strains of Vivaldi's *Spring*. The contrast could not have been greater.

The Tale of the Stubborn Donkey

I can only agree with the dictum coined in the entertainment business: "Don't ever work with children or animals." The pastoral care team of UnitingCare Ageing Central Coast was asked to contribute to a creative, outdoor Christmas celebration. We decided to produce a nativity play. We had Mary and Joseph, complete with a live baby. Our residents caught the spirit of the occasion and dressed as wise men, shepherds, and the angel Gabriel. We set the manger scene with live farm animals, which added authenticity.

All went swimmingly until the grand entrance of our live donkey, who was meant to accompany the holy family. The brown creature poked its nervous nose through the entrance, took stage fright, and stopped short. No amount of coaxing, nurturing, carrot-bribery, rope-pulling, or bottom-slapping could encourage the ass to move one inch.

Until that evening, I had little appreciation of the disproportionate size to strength ratio a donkey has. The poor thing became stressed and planted a number-two bodily offering on the carefully polished floor. Dustpan and broom hastily appeared. Plan B swiftly swung into action.

Mary and Joseph arrived, minus their four-footed friend, at the manger. The unfortunate beast was gently ushered away to munch on quieter green pastures, where later, little children were allowed to ride on its back.

The Tale of the Hot Sun

One day, I was soaking up the sun in my motorized wheelchair, whose wheels were fully pumped. Minding my own business in silent contemplation, I heard a mighty explosion. "So this is what the end of the world sounds like," I thought. I jumped out of my skin, and my heart thumped through my chest. My exaggerated startle response launched me into Neptune's orbit.

When I recovered, careering back to Earth space, I looked down to see that one of my back tyres had burst. What to do? I could not move. I called the NRMA, a local motoring organisation, on the mobile phone hanging round my neck. They repaired the flat in a jiffy.

The Tale of the Fallen Woman

Having carefully dressed to the nines in a long green skirt and a cream, feminine jumper, my hair exquisitely styled and face powder and lipstick applied with great attention, I thought I was the Queen of Sheba incarnate. This ephemeral dream shattered when I fell splat on my face while walking too slowly on my Canadian crutches through some fast automatic closing glass doors.

What was the occasion? A kind man I dated had shouted me to a meal to die for at the posh Wentworth Hotel in Sydney. Bang went the idea of a wannabe elegant, refined woman trying to attract him! Hotel staff scrambled from all directions to rescue the damsel in distress. I thought, "Get real, Heather. Impression creation doesn't work." With me, it is "What you see is what you get!"

The Tale of the Mistaken Words

As an aged-care chaplain, I was often privileged to hear stories of sadness and joy surrounding the lives of ageing people. On one occasion, an elderly lady was recounting to me with a serious expression the story of her husband's death. She informed me that he had suffered a heart attack and was lying on the floor until the paramedics arrived to offer assistance.

Her next words caused me a massive internal explosion of controlled mirth. My lips trembled with supreme effort as I tried to maintain the gravitas of the situation. Quite innocently, she explained, "The ambulance officers administered artificial insemination."

APPENDIX E

Acknowledging Personal Feelings and Relationships with Others

JUST AS A tradesperson requires a box of tools to get the job done, so a person with a disability needs to develop certain qualities and skills in order to run their marathon.

Personal Development

- If you tend to be on the pessimistic side in looking at the world, consider experimenting with two surprising strategies which may help foster a helpful attitude: "Fake it, until you make it" and "Act your way into the feeling." On the face of it, these pieces of advice hardly seem heroic, but they do have some scientific basis.

To illustrate: By nature, taking after my dad, I am more of a pessimist, struggling to see the positive. I am a Murphy's Law kind of gal. If anything can go wrong, it will.

Many of my acquaintances are surprised to hear this. They see my smile, my humour, and my positive attitude. It is true my outward expression is often a reflection of my inner life. But when the going gets tough, they do not see my struggle to rise above my natural negativity.

If I waited for a positive mood to appear, I could be waiting a while. So I encourage my body to do the action I want to achieve. If nervousness overtakes me, for example, I adopt a more open posture. I discipline my muscles to lift my head, pull back my shoulders, raise my eyes, smile, and engage in whatever task is required. Feelings of confidence and power increase following postural change.

A physiotherapist, Darren Stuchberry of 6S Health, informed me of a research study which confirms this strategy. I quote the journal article's abstract:

> Humans and other animals express power through open, expansive postures, and they express powerlessness through closed, contractive postures. But can these postures actually cause power? The results of this study confirmed our prediction that posing in high-power nonverbal displays (as opposed to low-power nonverbal displays) would cause neuroendocrine and behavioural changes for both male and female participants: High-power posers experienced elevations in testosterone, decreases in

cortisol, and increased feelings of power and tolerance for risk; low-power posers exhibited the opposite pattern. In short, posing in displays of power caused advantaged and adaptive psychological, physiological, and behavioural changes, and these findings suggest that embodiment extends beyond mere thinking and feeling, to physiology and subsequent behavioural choices. That a person can, by assuming two simple 1-min poses, embody power and instantly become more powerful has real-world, actionable implications.[1]

- On tough days, it is easy to fall into a rut of comparing your abilities unfavourably with the capacities of others. Natural though it may be, this attitude can eventually lead down the slippery slope into depression. When I am in that situation, I tell myself, "Be the person God truly made you to be. You can never be a photocopy of anyone else, no matter how noble or skilled they are."

To illustrate: There is a tale of the Hasidim related by Jewish philosopher, Martin Buber, which points to this reality beautifully.

A rabbi named Zusya died and went to stand before the judgment seat of God. As he waited for God to appear, he grew nervous thinking about his life and how little he had done. He began to imagine that God was going to ask him, "Why weren't you Moses or why weren't you Solomon or why weren't you David?"

But when God appeared, the rabbi was surprised. God simply asked, "Why weren't you Zusya?"[2]

- Tim McCallum, an Australian singer who happens to be a wheelchair user, has discovered that "your disability is only part of what defines and describes you. You are many things."[3]

I bring this understanding to my life: I am a Christian, an aspiring author, a daughter, a sister-in-law, an aunt, a friend, a classical music lover, a minister, a tutor, and a lover of nature. I am this and more. The way I express these values, relationships, and interests is shaped to some extent by my experience of cerebral palsy.

Your disability affects the expression of who you are, but it is definitely not the whole picture. You and I are far richer and deeper than our physical frames.

- If you are faced with a huge, impossible task, slice and dice the task into small, manageable bits. Creighton Abrams, a US Army general, said, "When you eat an elephant, take one bite at a time."[4]

Further, if my elephant is an administrative task and I am sitting at my desk, overwhelmed by mountains of demands screaming at me, I make an effort to remove from my sight all extraneous scraps of paper. In this way, I concentrate only on the couple of documents relating to the first and most important task in front of me.

To illustrate: Having procrastinated for a year on starting to write this book, I began with simply creating a computer folder for writing projects. Next day, I wrote a few headings. Even those small actions helped to eliminate the paralysis of gazing at a blank page. Next day, I numbered the pages. The following day, I placed under each heading some scattered thoughts, not worrying initially about sentence structure or creating a literary masterpiece. Momentum increases with action.

- Do what you easily can, to optimise and strengthen your abilities.

- Develop an attitude of gratitude. List the good things that have happened at the end of the day. Let the good overwhelm the tough, as far as possible.

- Set manageable and achievable goals for yourself. Even if you don't get there fast, you have a plan to motivate you. Clear, precise thoughts can improve the likelihood of getting where you would like to be.

- Keep your eye on the imagined joy of the goal you want to achieve, rather than the sheer effort of the process.

To illustrate: While I was serving as an aged care chaplain in Gerringong, I used to visit sick residents in the local hospitals. I received great satisfaction from being with people in vulnerable situations. However, to fulfil this enriching pastoral activity, I walked slowly to my car, grunted my way into the Mazda, drove for half an hour, operated my wheelchair hoist to lower my wheelchair from the roof of my vehicle to the ground, assembled the chair, transferred from car to wheelchair, wheeled my manual chair along corridors to the ward where the patient was, and then repeated the procedure in reverse after the visit. This was an enormous effort, to be sure. There were times I thought, "Is it worth it?" The answer sneaked up on me in the warm appreciation of the residents. Perhaps in a small way, my visit made a positive difference in the life of a fellow struggler.

Here is a story from an unknown source. A young boy in a remote community walked miles to give his teacher a gift of a beautiful seashell. The teacher was expansive in her praise of this gesture. She exclaimed "But you have come so far!"

"Don't worry, miss. The journey is part of the gift."

- Beyond a reasonable wish to extend your physical boundaries, remember that you live your life to the beat of a different drum as compared to people who can run the four-minute mile. In a wise little booklet titled "Slow-Down Therapy," there is a delightful quote which has encouraged me: "Direct your life with purposeful choices, not with speed and efficiency. The best musician is the one who plays with expression and meaning, not the one who finishes first."[5]

- There is more than one way to craft a life. Just because someone does something one way does not mean you may only carry it out exactly the same way. Daring to be different can enhance your creativity. Whether you use assistive devices or not, open your mind to alternative ways of doing ordinary chores. I personally find chins very handy for stabilizing or carrying some objects.

Emotional Care

- Courage does not equate with not being scared. Courage is keeping on with a worthwhile task, even when your knees knock and your hands tremble. I like the saying, "Courage does not always roar."[6] Often it is clothed in quiet, unnoticed acts of faithfulness, especially when one does not feel like doing them.

- Anger can often be released with physical activity. Punching a pillow, running or walking (if you are able), and doing your exercises are possibilities.

- Train your mind to think as positively as you are able at the time. It is so easy to limit the possibilities for your future by the focusing disproportionately on the enervating challenges of today. I once heard of a man suffering many physical problems. He used to say to others, "Tomorrow will be a better day."

There is also a useful quotation which may originally have been a Chinese proverb, first cited in Western circles in W.

L. Watkinson's sermon "The Invincible Strategy," collected in 1907: "Yet is it better to light a candle than to curse the darkness."[7] In other words, In the face of bad times or hopelessness, it is more worthwhile to do some good, however small, than to complain about the situation.

- If someone underestimates your ability to do a task you are skilled at and declines your offer, it can be hurtful. What I have discovered is that more time is needed to build the trust level, so they can develop a more realistic assessment of who you are and what you are capable of doing. Patience is an underrated virtue.

- If you want to make sense of the chaos in your mind, there is no shame in going to a skilled counsellor. On a number of occasions, I have done just that. Healing is possible in the presence of an empathic person who understands you deeply and can often point to realities that you are blind to at that moment.

- If you are frustrated and angry, try journaling. Write or type your feelings honestly. Let your diary be your confessor. Let your fire spark from the page. Alternatively, channel your passion into constructive activity. Let your anger work for you.

- Acknowledge the grief and loss in your life with trusted friends. With their help, you may be able to see the gift in your suffering. I am struck deeply by these words from Nicholas Wolterstorff: "I shall look at the world through tears. Perhaps I shall see things that, dry-eyed, I could not see."[8]

Nurturing Your Relationships

- While we cannot take responsibility for other people's feelings or reactions towards our disability, at least we can be aware of how hard it is for them.

To illustrate: A friend was helping me into the car. As usual, I was having difficulty with the routine. With honesty I admire, he said, "I am suffering to see you struggle. I don't know how to deal with it. I am a male used to having to fix things, and I cannot fix this." After encouraging him by saying he had a compassionate heart, I suggested that he might like to disassemble my wheelchair and put the parts in my car while I finished my struggle. I believe that was a constructive way through the dilemma.

- Learn from my mistakes. Occasionally, the urge to have a deep and meaningful encounter comes on me quickly. My timing, however, leaves much to be desired. For example, involved conversations on the refugee crisis cannot occur when a poor friend is struggling to assemble the footplates on my wheelchair.

- Take a friendly interest in your carers' and other friends' lives. They are people too. Give of yourself. Don't only let yourself be on the receiving end. Listen lovingly to the message behind the words. The philosopher Philo of Alexandria said, "Be kind to all, because everyone is fighting a great battle."[9]

- Having a disability means that sometimes you are at the mercy of another's timetable, waiting for doctors, carers, and other busy people who are capable of engaging in activities you are unable to. Sometimes you can feel abandoned or useless, like a pimple on a pumpkin. Life whizzes by and you are forced to stay put.

The practice of waiting, though, can develop into an art form. I make sure that I have a book in tow or a notepad and pen. Knitting is another activity which fills waiting minutes. Unobtrusive physical exercises use the time creatively. On other occasions I pray, perhaps for people in my current field of vision, such as the postman as he roars by on his motorbike, having delivered my letters.

When waiting in shopping centres, the process of observing passers-by can be highly entertaining and sometimes educational. I have learned a lot about fashion—what works and what does not! Attending mindfully to the colours, the volume, the feelings, and the people around you can stretch your mind, imagination and capacity to empathise with the struggles of bustling humanity.

- Stephanie Dowrick, a multi-faith minister practising in Sydney, New South Wales, quoted on Facebook the words of Anne Frank, a young Jewish girl who hid from the Nazis during World War II: "A single candle can both defy and define the darkness."

Stephanie's Facebook post on kindness continues. She says:

Please never underestimate what a vast difference a small act of kindness may make in someone's life, especially if they are feeling fragile or in any way lost. The light of kindness can literally lead us out of darkness. It can take us 'home' to a more secure sense of ourselves.

Sometimes that act of kindness is, in essence, an act of mindful restraint: NOT saying or doing something that could in any way be hurtful; silencing any bitterness, self-pity or criticism; not putting someone 'right'.

Even when life is good and we are feeling robust, it is kindness, appreciation and encouragement that keep us most happily connected. Those treasures are yours to give. And yours to receive gracefully."

- If you are housebound, invite friends to come to you. Often they are willing to make a pot of tea or bring goodies.

To illustrate: When I finally purchased from my employer the house that I had been living in for twelve years, my friends suggested we have a house-warming party. I was enthusiastic. Some agreed to prepare the space half an hour before the occasion. Another friend bought a large cake beautifully decorated. On top were the words "Happy Home, Heather" with a chocolate-ice drawing of a house with smoke rising from the chimney. How generous! There were echoes of Jesus's parables likening the kingdom of heaven to feasts of celebration. The party-loving, unseen Guest was certainly present with us that day.

- Simone Weil, French philosopher, Christian mystic, and social activist expresses the importance of listening, "Attention is the rarest and purest form of generosity."[10]

  Jonathan Foer, as a commentator on her work, has this to say: "Most of the time, most people are not crying in public, but everyone is in need of something that someone else can give, be it undivided attention, a kind word or deep empathy. There is no better use of a life than to be attentive to such needs."[11]

  Deep listening is powerful. One of my battles has been to learn how not to judge others whose behaviour I find difficult. Sometimes, if I make the effort to listen carefully to people I find hard to relate to, I will stumble over an "aha" experience which doubles my awareness of why they behave the way they do. Often, difficult behaviour is a natural response to great hurt.

  Some of the peak experiences in my life have happened when people truly and deeply listened to my story. I have been incredibly moved when people wept with me. Focused, caring listening is vital for cherishing your friends and family. In this way, icy hearts may start to melt.

- Although mixing with able-bodied people for a large slice of life broadens one's horizons, there is a definite place for keeping in touch with companions who have disabilities too. I have valued conversations on occasions with those who have lived experience of impairment. There can be sheer relief in sharing with those who know what it is like. There is a bond that can form when you don't have to explain.

To illustrate: For a while, after feeling weak from stints in hospital, I subscribed to a Christian devotional website targeted to people with chronic illness, Rest Ministries at *http://restministries.com/*

While I recovered from lack of energy and muscle de-conditioning, I found reading about others' experiences of weakness was strangely comforting. Connecting with fellow strugglers was therapeutic in this enforced time of "floating." I had no energy left for striving.

- If you are on the verge of launching your career, consider voluntary work in the approximate field in which you wish to work. The networks and the job skills you can potentially acquire will be very helpful.

APPENDIX F

Coping with Pain, Discomfort, and ther Physical Situations

Fitness

Regular physiotherapy and exercise loosen my muscles. Fitness has always loomed large among my priorities to help maintain my energy. If I don't keep a regular routine, my muscles tighten quickly. I have a positive, energetic team working with me.

Physios have often said "Keep breathing, Heather" when I have held my breath to exert my body into action. I could never seem to master this necessary technique until finally an exercise physiologist told me, "Breathe out before effort." Here was a specific technique to optimise my energy and to relieve the pressure of holding my breath. At long last, it made sense.

Warm-up exercises and stretches, followed by interval training on my walking frame, seem to work well for me at the moment. These routines tax every ounce of strength I have, leaving me heaving for breath. In fact, one of the clinical measurements my therapist uses is the degree to which my breath fogs up my glasses! I notice small improvements on good days, but I strive for consistency. Mood, amount of sleep, oedema, time of day, temperature, verbal encouragement from the therapist, and setting of specific, measurable goals all affect my performance on a given day.

If my land exercise requires exceptional discipline and mental focus, then swimming and other hydrotherapy in a heated pool is sheer fun-filled delight. At the very least, there is less pressure on my sore joints.

Nurturing Your Body

- There is no shame in rest, especially if you have had a hard day. There are just some times when you don't feel like being the all-conquering superhero!

  Neuroscientist Sarah McKay writes about brain health on her website *Everyday Neuroscience for Brain Health and Wellness*. In her words:

  > A good night sleep every night should be a priority, not a luxury. Sleep is overlooked, underappreciated, and the number one, fundamental bedrock of good health. Sleep deprivation (even a few hours a night) impacts cognition (thinking), mood, memory and learning and leads to chronic disease.
  >
  > Sleep is essential for consolidating memories and for draining waste products from the brain. Not only do we under-sleep, we under-consume natural light during the day and over-consume artificial

light at night leaving our natural circadian rhythms, hormones and immune systems dysregulated.

Short afternoon naps consolidate memory, spark creativity and smooth your rough emotional edges (no guru, course or app required!).[1]

- Work out at the time of day you experience your peak energy flow. Do your most demanding work when you are feeling on top of the world, and slow down when your body tires.

- Severe pain can be debilitating, jangling, and screeching. It can make you cranky and hard to live with. Talk to your health professionals about it. But don't continually harp on your pain with those you live and work with. People get tired of it and feel helpless. At one stage I naively thought that pain would eventually go away with appropriate treatment. Instead I am now learning to live with treated pain.

- Pain can intensify if the rest of life is out of balance. I believe that if our relationships are not life-giving, if our general health is not nurtured, if resentment is eating us, if our spirit life is not fed, then these situations have a negative effect on some kinds of pain. I am not saying that all pain will disappear when one lives a life that is as ordered as it can be. But being physically, emotionally, relationally, and spiritually healthy certainly strengthens one's capacity to cope.

- Appropriate medical pain management, distraction, looking out for the needs of others, showering under warm water, soaking up the sun, and watching comedy on television may be helpful strategies for making pain tolerable. Laughter, in fact, can be good medicine because it releases feel-good hormones called *endorphins* into your body.

- Take responsibility of the directions of your health care and social support. Don't wait for others to make decisions for you. Ask questions.

- Keep your fitness up for as long as you are able, even if the only thing you move is your little finger. Swimming and other exercise are good ways to channel frustrations.

- Your unique body shape or its volume may not be within your capacity to control. When your capacity to exercise is limited, this factor complicates life a little. However, healthy nutrition is within your reach to enjoy. As one who delights in chocolate from time to time (there, that's my confession!), I still appreciate the need to limit sugar in my diet. Too much junk food can lead to added kilojoules and a wide circumference! Excess weight can make already difficult movement even more strenuous, and puts additional strain on existing dodgy joints and heart. More flab makes your carer's task more difficult too. (Boy, I am starting to sound like the food police!)

Clothes, Shoes, and Equipment

Clothes

Fashion is a very personal choice. These are simply observations that have worked well for me.

- Buying online can sometimes work, because you can try on clothes in the comfort of your own home instead of manoeuvring a wheelchair in claustrophobic dressing rooms.

- If you use a manual wheelchair, minimise your use of cream or white long-sleeved blouses and jumpers, because mud rubbed from your wheelchair wheels is much more conspicuous.

- Wear loose-fitting clothes, which are much more comfortable to get on and off. Stretchy fabric has more give in dressing manoeuvres.

- Watches, beads, necklaces, and bangles without fiddly clasps are preferable.

- Slacks can potentially be easier for toileting as compared to dresses and skirts. They can also act as a barrier against mosquitoes, cover swollen limbs, and disguise ugly leg braces.

- Minimise back or side fastenings, which can be fiddly. I personally find zippered fronts on slacks are preferable to elastic waists, which can be pulled down unexpectedly. When I am transferring, zippers can prevent embarrassing "wardrobe malfunctions."

- Buttons on blouses and shirts may make an enjoyable change, but throw-over tops are less time-consuming to put on.

- Dark colours can be slimming and can often cover stains. Vertical stripes, if you are larger, can be flattering, whereas lateral stripes can make you look bigger than you are.

- Buy low maintenance, no-iron clothes where possible. They can assist in either your carer's energy and time management, or yours.

Petal Back Clothing is a range of assistive clothing for people with mobility limitations. I have not personally tried the company's products, but it may be worth checking out their website: *www.petalback-clothing.com*

- I encourage you to not pack away in mothballs your special clothes, your jewellery, or your dancing shoes—items which, in your mind, can only be worn on royal occasions. Remember, each day can be a day to celebrate with appropriate panache.

- Don't be afraid to look stylish. Clothes are not *the* definer of a person, but when you look good and foster a neat exterior, it can give your sense of self-worth a bit of a boost. Style and colour do not have to be expensive or ostentatious. Whether we like it or not, first impressions do count, until people realise we are more than our clothes. It shows others that we care about ourselves.

To illustrate: I recently attended a seminar on disability. I engaged in conversation with a woman whom I had never met. She happened to be a motorised wheelchair user like myself. Impeccably groomed, she wore a colourful green outfit, had tasteful make-up, and sported a pearl-like bracelet on her wrist. I thought, "This is a lady to be taken seriously!" We do not have to wear Christian Dior, but we can look our best within our means.

Shoes

Allow me the luxury of drawing upon a childhood recollection about shoes which illustrates a necessary balance between function and beauty.

I am ten years old, visiting Ma and Pa, my grandparents. From a seated position, I proudly swing my legs backward and forward to show off my new black party shoes, complete with stylish instep straps. I giggle with delight because this is my first pair of decorative footwear. Until now, I have only had big, brown orthopaedic boots which very sensibly support my weak ankles as I walk. These boots are cumbersome clodhoppers which do nothing to enhance my sense of "feeling pretty," to use an Eliza Doolittle phrase from the musical *My Fair Lady*. My party shoes, so shiny I can see my face in them, are a celebration of feeling free from the things I do that are simply sensible.

From that pleasant sojourn in the channels of memory, we return to the practicalities of footwear.

- Velcro straps on shoes are easier than laces for some of us to secure.

- Some shoes are made of stretch material to allow room for feet to swell.

- If you have trouble bending down to remove shoes, metal eyelets may be fitted to shoe straps. Eyelets enable a long-handled hook to slide through the hole and pull the strap in order to loosen the footwear.

- Long-handled shoehorns may make life a little easier.

Equipment

- When buying assistive devices, make sure your supplier has reliable, prompt after-sales service.

  To illustrate: My motorised bed chucked a wobbly. Instead of descending to enable me to transfer to the mattress, the upper part of the bed hummed bolt upright in a seated position, despite my frantic jiggles of buttons on the remote control. This movement made it impossible for me to achieve a lying-down position.

The service technician made a two-hour car journey to fix it, arriving at ten thirty at night, so that I wouldn't have to sleep upright in my wheelchair. This is customer service second to none. He was an angel on the night shift.[2]

Physical Tips for Wheelies

- Buy portable battery lights and/or torches in preparation for electricity blackouts. Tie them, if possible, to your wheelchair or around your neck.

- Transfer from wheelchair to bed, toilet, or other chair from a higher level to a lower level where possible. Use gravity to work for you.

- Breathe out before any major physical effort. I find this relieves the pressure in your head caused by extended holding of breath. A purple face, I find, is not a good look!

- Align a specific, prescribed exercise with a specific activity you do during the day. For example, I try to straighten my shoulders each time I wheel down the hallway of my home.

- Take your regular pain medications half an hour before major physical effort.

- Write a list of questions to ask your doctor. In the stress of the moment during an appointment, you might forget (if you are anything like me).

- Make decisions easier for your family and friends by informing them of your wishes for your health care needs. Arrange for an advance care directive, and make a will. Appoint power of attorney for financial provision and enduring guardian for health decisions. These strategies will help in the eventuality that you are unable to communicate your decisions and preferences for your future.

- If government-sponsored e-health records are available where you are, consider enrolling in the scheme to minimise repetition of your medical history to numerous health professionals. Of course, check out the privacy safeguards for the system.

Physical Tips for Able-Bodied Friends

If you are a friend of a person with disability and want to assist, you might be thinking, "Help, am I doing or saying the right thing? I feel like a klutz." Rest assured, if you are genuinely trying to listen carefully and have a teachable attitude and a sincere desire to build a relationship, then you are more than halfway there. "What do you need?" is a great question to ask. Hopefully, the following pointers will help too.

- Sit at eye level with a person in a wheelchair. Don't let them crane their neck. It can also be a psychological disadvantage for them to always be looking up at others.

  To illustrate: I will never forget my friend who, during her wedding reception, glided around to speak with me. She looked magnificent in her glittering gown. Kneeling down in front of my wheelchair, she gracefully sat on the floor and looked up at me. Her dress arranged itself naturally in a voluminous circle of white fabric. That simple act of humility, in the midst of her bridal glory, moved me greatly.

- If you are wheeling a person's manual chair, and another person stops you for conversation, turn the chair around so the person in the chair can be included in the chat.

- Watch the speed if you are wheeling a person in a manual wheelchair. Running too fast can be dizzying, especially when negotiating corners. Plodding slowly is like watching the grass grow. If in doubt, ask.

- If you see a wheelie struggling to get something from the top shelf in a supermarket, offer to reach it for them.

- Ask what the person wants in terms of assistance. Do no more or less until you consult.

- If you are unsure of whether to offer help, give both options in your approach: "Do you want help, or are you OK by yourself?"

- If you are helping with housework, return any items you have moved to their original spots. Many a time, when a friend has left I have been unable to reach items I needed. Sometimes it is not as important, like putting my favourite snack of potato chips in a top cupboard (!). Other times, it is crucial. For example, placing walking sticks in an inaccessible spot may be likened to unwittingly chopping your friend's legs off.

- If you are refrigerating food, packing crockery away, or finding a home for bags, make sure the items are still in reach for your wheelie friend.

- If you are phoning or ringing the doorbell, allow extra time for a response.

APPENDIX G

Tending to Your Mind

and Attitudes

Nurturing your Mind

I LIKE THE wisdom of this Native American parable. An old Cherokee was teaching his grandson about life. "A fight is going on inside me," he said. "It is a terrible fight, and it is between two wolves. One is evil—he is anger, envy, sorrow, regret, greed, arrogance, self-pity, guilt, resentment, inferiority, lies, false pride, superiority, and ego. The other is good—he is joy, peace, love, hope, serenity, humility, kindness, benevolence, empathy, generosity, truth, compassion, and faith. The same fight is going on inside you—and inside every other person too."

The grandson thought about it for a minute and then asked, "Which wolf will win?"

The old Cherokee replied simply, "The one you feed."[1]

What strikes me about this story is the importance of choice in determining what kind of attitudes we foster in our lives. Between an event which happens and one's response to it, there is a significant gap, within which one's mind chooses its own direction. Kindness, for example, can take the heat out of a potential conflict. Alternatively, an act of revenge can, in the blink of an eye, deepen the chasm of misunderstanding between fragile people.

How can we nourish our minds? Strategies include looking after the physical health of our bodies, and choosing the quality of books we read, TV we watch, and social media in which we engage.

Another major factor in shaping our attitudes is the influence of our friends and associates. Our heroes, heroines, role models, and peer groups have great potential to either build us up or suck the life out of us. The mind is a precious gift which has huge potential for good, but it needs to be fed with great nutrients.

- Read if possible. This activity keeps the brain active and engaged. If you don't use it, you lose it. I firmly believe that if your physical life is limited, a journey into books, magazines, e-books, and audiotapes expands your horizons. With the help of a book, you can go to places in your imagination that your body cannot take you.

- Before launching into a difficult manoeuvre, such as an exercise routine, imagine success first. Visualise yourself completing the end goal before you even start. I recall a story about a golfer who visualized making successful putts while he was in prison. Upon his release, even though he had not physically practised, he was able to down great shots on the golf course.

- Sometimes I find an affirmation like "I can do this" puts me in a better frame of mind for a difficult task.

- Keep abreast of current affairs and health information. The Internet is a real boost, especially for people with disability. Caution, however, needs to be exercised in discerning the authenticity and quality of the information. Not all advice on the net is true or helpful.

- I have often wished for a more spontaneous life. In my fantasy, I would love to be able to walk up to the shops just when I want, to buy a carton of milk. Simple, really. The reality, though, is that I need to plan everything, to make the most of my carer's limited time or to make the most of my energy levels. Wasted energy is minimised. I am a copious list maker in an effort to optimise energy efficiency.

- However, the rebel in me sometimes ditches the list to alleviate my feelings of guilt when I do not complete tasks. Use the list if it helps. Discard it when it is a chain around your neck.

- Life has some hard patches, especially for people with disability and their families. Few know just how teeth-grittingly difficult specific challenges are. Don't give up. I am surprised at the lack of staying power I see in some people. Dare to be a living example of sheer gutsiness. You don't have to say anything. Just keep on keeping on.

  To illustrate: In my office, there used to hang a cartoon of a desperate frog about to be breakfast for a hungry bird. There he was, strangling the neck of a pelican in order to get his head out of its gulping bill. The caption: "Never give up!"

Tips for Able-Bodied Friends

- Encourage people with disability to make decisions whenever possible. This process is empowering,

- Genuinely encourage strength rather than focusing on weakness. Albert Einstein, physicist, had a witty saying to drive home this point: "Everyone is a genius, but if you judge a fish by its ability to climb a tree, it will live its whole life believing that it is stupid."[2]

- Unless you are a health professional conducting a medical assessment, do not continually draw attention to the faults or weaknesses in your friend's body. It is the only one they have. They are surprisingly attached to it, imperfect though it might be. Even if you have to professionally assess a person with a disability, there are sensitive ways in which to explain what is going on without using denigrating words.

- However, do not idealise people with disability or put them up on a pedestal, which can in fact be isolating. They have faults and failings like everyone else. If they explode in frustration occasionally, validate their feelings. "You are having a bad day and you are feeling lousy" is often a helpful response. It can provide a safe space to express what is difficult.

  To illustrate: I am a devil at 6:30 a.m., when I struggle out of bed. My brother once gave me a mug with the Peanuts cartoon dog Snoopy etched on it. With dark circles under his eyes, Snoopy is lying flat on the roof of his kennel, looking depleted and the worse for wear. The caption reads "I think I am allergic to morning." Touché!

- Take the time to get to know a person deeply, in such a way that the disability becomes secondary. Buried treasure is there to be discovered. Initially you may feel uncomfortable in your attempts to communicate, but it is worth the effort in the long run.

  To illustrate: A former boss told me this story. He took the time to converse with an intelligent speech-impaired man. Because of the effort involved in expressing and understanding, the man could only enunciate three or four sentences. In the space of an hour's conversation, my boss discovered that the man was a devoted fan of the author Charles Dickens. Not only that, it was the first time in a long while that the man had been asked a question beyond the superficial level of "Do you take sugar in your tea?"

- Do not make the assumption, in planning group activities for people with disability that they will automatically connect easily to another with a similar condition. It could be that a person with disability has more in common with an able-bodied person who has a shared interest in footy or gardening, for example.

- If you are accompanying someone with a disability on a shopping trip, and the shopkeeper directs a question to you which is more appropriate for your companion, face your friend say something like, "I am sure So-and-So is able to help you with that query." The barriers are crumbling, little by little, but some able-bodied people still feel overawed by speaking directly to a person with a disability.

- If you are going on a holiday or to a recreational event with your friend with a disability, it is far more respectful and less patronising to say "So-and-So and I are going on a holiday together" rather than "I am taking So-and-So on a holiday." Language has the potential to be empowering.

Employment Aspects

- If you are in a position to employ workers in your organisation, consider taking on an appropriately skilled person with a disability. Forge links with agencies specialising in placing those who have impairments. Employees with disabilities are often loyal and reliable. Because the employment market is so competitive for us, we have to prove our capacities and qualities much more. In Australia, at least, there are government incentives to assist employers in this educational experience.

Carer Experience

- If you are a full-time or part-time carer of a person with a disability, self-care is important for long-term survival. Caring can be exhausting, both physically and emotionally. You are often unsung heroes and heroines. If the reserves in your energy tank are low, then resentment can unwittingly surface. This is not ultimately good for the relationship. Take responsibility for your own breaks and breathers. There are often carer respite services available in your local area to offer you options.

APPENDIX H

Nurturing Your Spirit As You Cope with Disability

THERE ARE DIFFERENT ways of strengthening the fire of the spirit within you. Here are a few observations to keep the flames stoked.

- I see the whimsical wisdom in this devotional piece:

> Hanging on tooth and nail can pull
> out your teeth and nails.
> One aspect of wisdom is knowing
> when to hang on …
> and when to let go.[1]

In the past, I admit that one of my strategies for survival has been "If anything fails, try harder." That may work in many situations, but in others, floating and surrendering is the best option. Going with the flow is worth a shot, especially when the doors ahead of you continually shut and you are getting angry and tired. Is God trying to teach you something? "Muddy waters, let stand, become clear."[2]

Quietness in order to discern divine whispers can often be more productive than charging like a bull in the proverbial china shop towards the first available option.

To illustrate: Upon retirement, fellow chaplains gave me a gift of great symbolic value. Knowing my love of swimming, and acknowledging that each of us had experienced challenging moments, they gave me a set of plastic arm-floaties to remind me that in the midst of turbulent waves, the best solution is often just to float instead of struggle.

- Pray to God honestly—for calmness, for a sense of humour, for a wider picture, for strength just to take the next step. Pray when you can do no more, when you reach the end of your rope. Remember to pray your thanks too.

Prayer can be one word uttered before God: "Help!" Some people pray with meditative music, others with pictures, icons, or candles to help them focus. Prayer can be contemplative silence or a rage of words. You can pray alone or in the enveloping love of caring friends or family.

There are times when I am too tired to pray. One of my mentors suggested, "Offer to God your tiredness. That is your prayer."

The Benedictine monk John Chapman wrote these encouraging words. "Pray as you can, not as you can't."[3]

I find simple breath prayers helpful, using short Bible verses. On your in breath, for example, pray, "Perfect love." On the exhalation, pray, "Casts out fear." Repeat five times or more, if helpful. Other succinct Bible phrases like "God be merciful to me a sinner" are a possible focus for breathed prayer.

- Sometimes I have received great strength from shared, prayerful silence. Even though there may be five or six people in a prayer group, there can be a sense of strong undergirding in community quietness before God.

To illustrate: I attended a Quaker worship meeting in Canberra. For the most part the meeting was conducted in silence with only an occasional word from a member who wished to share wisdom with the wider group. While I missed the experience of a sermon, Bible reading, and music, I realised again that corporate silence can heighten my awareness and senses to the needs of the world. To this day, I remember a little girl running up to me after the meeting. She gave me a little white chrysanthemum to share the occasion of Mother's Day. The spontaneity of the gift had a beautiful clarity that I might have missed had I not experienced the previous silence.

- One of many prayers I love is the Serenity Prayer by Reinhold Neibuhr, a North American theologian. You might like to pray it when you are trying to discern the best way forward in a dilemma.

> God, grant me the serenity to accept the things
> I cannot change, The courage to change the things
> I can, And the wisdom to know the difference.[4]

- Another kind of prayer is simply receiving God's gifts in thankfulness. I love bushwalking. This activity provides ample opportunity to use all my senses to enjoy beauty. Take your time to survey the scene. Feel the warmth of the sun on your skin. See the fine veins of a small leaf, or a mauve flower which defies all reason and blossoms where there seems to be no hope of life. Thank God for the ability to hear the flap of a bird's wings.

- Don't exhaust yourself on trying to do *everything* yourself. Keep some energy for doing the things you enjoy. Life is also about fun and contributing to society, not just about survival.

- Savour beautiful memories to nurture your soul in times of difficulty.

To illustrate: I hold in my memory the image of running with a girlfriend on a beach as she pushed me in a wheelchair beach buggy. In a moment of exuberance, we charged with great gusto into an unsuspecting flock of seagulls standing peacefully on the sand. Within the space of seconds, they flew into the sky. I remember the sound of their drumming wings. We looked up in wonder at their beauty as the flock flew into the sparkling sun, surrounded by clear blue sky.

- Find beauty around you, even though you might be climbing a metaphorical mountain.

To illustrate: A mentor shared her wisdom with me after I complained to her that I had huge mountains to climb in life. She said, "That may be true, but enjoy the wildflowers on the way."

Some of my "wildflowers" include enjoying simple things like rainbow lorikeets and blue wrens, bright yellow daffodils, cascades of lavender-coloured wisteria, colourful sunsets painted by the Master Artist, star-gazing on a clear night, a full moon with a striking resemblance to a shiny gold sovereign in the night sky, fragrant perfume, light classical music, hugs, strawberry milkshakes, massages, fictional murder mysteries, and inspiring biographies. You can tell I delight in the use of my senses.

- If you can't get out much, surround yourself with a beautiful garden, asking friends or gardeners to help. If your budget does not stretch to creating a garden to rival those of Versailles right away, follow your dream in stages.

To illustrate: To kick-start the beautification of my garden, which had become a wild jungle, Mum planted red geraniums. This action alone added a splash of colour to an otherwise grey paling fence.

I also employed a gardener to plant new plants. We installed an irrigation system with a timer so the whole garden is watered simultaneously. For able-bodied people, this achievement may not seem much. For me, being able to water my pretty nature patch with one flick of the tap is an instance of joyful empowerment.

- When your energy is low and your resources are few, remember that the creativity of God can multiply your efforts, if we offer to God the little we have.

To illustrate: I am encouraged by the story of Jesus feeding five thousand people (Matt. 14:13–21). He is faced with the hunger of a massive crowd and only has at his disposal five loaves and two fish. He prays to God in blessing, food is shared, and they are all fed. What seems an impossible task becomes manageable when we offer the little we have to get the ball rolling. Christian tradition affirms that when the odds are against us, God's strength prevails if we offer our availability to his bigger purposes.

- Remember, we receive much in our lives, but there is also joy in giving what we have to offer. People with disability often know what it is like to live on limited incomes. Our physical impairments sometimes mean that we have great medical expenses, and either work part-time or are recipients of a pension. Even though we often live with less money, I believe it is part of our responsibility to give to those who are less well off than we are.

One of my favourite gospel stories is about the widow's offering, found in Luke: "As Jesus looked up, he saw the rich putting their gifts into the temple treasury. He also saw a poor widow put in two very small copper coins. 'Truly I tell you,' he said, 'this poor widow has put in more than all the others. All these people gave their gifts out of their wealth; but she out of her poverty put in all she had to live on'" (21:1–4 NIV).

What I love about this story is the woman's generosity even in scarcity. Giving to others energises us. Seeing other people benefit can give us breath for our marathon as well as theirs.

- Giving is not only related to material possessions. It is also sharing our time or experience. I believe we as people with disability have an educational role in increasing understanding among both children and adults.

To illustrate: If you, as a wheelchair user, are in a shopping centre, and a little child runs to you and asks, "Why are you in a wheelchair?" take a stab at answering the question. I start the conversation with the words, "Because my legs don't work properly," and then I see where that leads us. Usually their poor, embarrassed mothers do not know which way to look. Honestly, I do not mind building a child's learning about disability. It is a great investment in their future and a small step to heightening awareness.

- Read about inspirational people to enrich your life. I need heroes and heroines to encourage me through joys and adversities. Whether they are people whom I know in person, or they come alive in history, I value role models to breathe life into me (the true meaning of *inspiration*). I do not need them to be perfect or too good to be true. I admire them because, despite flaws, they possess qualities I want to emulate.

Abraham Lincoln (1809–1865)

One of the values I appreciate in this former president of the United States is his perseverance in failure.

Tony Alessandra recounts part of Lincoln's story which underlines his dogged determination:

In 1832, Lincoln was working in a general store in Illinois when he decided to run for the state legislature. However, the election was some months away, and before it took place, the store went bankrupt and Lincoln was out of a job. He joined the army for three months. When he left, it was time for the election—which he lost.

Then, with a partner, Lincoln opened a new general store. His partner embezzled from the business, and the store went broke. Shortly after, the partner died, leaving Lincoln with debts that took several years to pay off. Lincoln ran again for the state legislature, and this time he won. He was elected to three more terms. During this period, Lincoln suffered severe depression.

Lincoln became a licensed attorney and later a diligent circuit-riding lawyer, travelling from county to county in Illinois to plead cases in different jurisdictions.

He was defeated in an attempt to become speaker of the Illinois legislature. He failed in a first attempt to win nomination for Congress. In 1846, he was elected to Congress, but in 1848, he had to leave because his party had a policy of limiting terms. In 1854, he was defeated in a run for the Senate. In 1856, he lost the nomination for vice president, and in 1858, he was again defeated in a race for the Senate.

Yet in spite of all these setbacks, in 1860 he was elected president of the United States.[5]

When I am tempted to give up, I look at Lincoln's lion-hearted spirit and feel rejuvenated.

Mother Teresa of Calcutta (1910–1997)

This compassionate nun rose to world fame because of her work with the poor and dying in Calcutta. However, publicity did not sit comfortably with her. Her signature strength was her humility, as shown in one of her sayings: "We can be little pencils in the hand of God."[6] She did not want to build monuments to human achievement, instead urging: "We do not have to do great things, only small things with great love."[7] What more do we know of this woman? I am indebted to Richard Rohr for supplying the following information.[8]

Mother Teresa was born in Macedonia, lived thirty years in Yugoslavia, and spent the balance of her life in India, serving the poorest of the poor. She founded the Missionaries of Charity, which provides homes, medical care, food, counselling, education, and more to the impoverished and sick.

Why am I drawn to this little woman with a giant spirit? I am inspired by her efforts to achieve a balance between praying and acting. These dimensions are intertwined closely, and each gives strength to the other. I am also moved by her self-giving spirit, which was not dimmed by the ruggedness of vulnerability she found in the faces of those she served. Speaking of her personal encounters with sick and dying people, she said, "Accept Jesus as he comes into your life and recognise him once more when he comes to you in his most distressing disguise."[9]

Dietrich Bonhoeffer (1906–1945)

Bonhoeffer, a Christian writer, lived during the time of Nazism in Germany. His anti-Nazi beliefs and actions led to his imprisonment for treason. A deep-thinking man, Dietrich was also a pastorally sensitive clergyman. While in prison, he encouraged his fellow inmates and warders. Sadly, he was executed by his captors only days before the American liberation.

I cannot but be moved by words he penned while incarcerated. The final stanza of his heartfelt prayer, "Who Am I?" speaks to the very depths of my being.

> Who am I? This or the other?
> Am I one person today and tomorrow another?
> Am I both at once? A hypocrite before others,
> And before myself a contemptibly woebegone weakling?
> Or is something within me still like a beaten army,
> Fleeing in disorder from victory already achieved?
> Who am I? They mock me, these lonely questions of mine.
> Whoever I am, Thou knowest, O God, I am Thine![10]

Like Bonhoeffer who experienced strength and weakness as a prisoner, I know what it is to feel strong one day and fragile the next. When I am faced with confusion, sometimes the only certainty I have is that I am beloved and held firmly by the Divine. Surely that is enough.

General William Booth (1829–1912)

The valiant warrior General William Booth founded of the Salvation Army and was renowned for his work among the poor. His son Bramwell one day had to break the news that his father would never see again. When the old man realised that a final darkness has descended, he grasped his son's hand and said, "Bramwell, I have done what I could for God and the people with my eyes. Now I shall do what I can without my eyes."[11]

What strikes me about this man was his utter willingness to be available to God and those around him with whatever capacities were still at his disposal. I crave that spirit of surrender.

Bibliography

Barclay, William. *The Gospel of Matthew. Volume 1: Chapters 1–10* Revised edition Edinburgh: St Andrews, 1975

Beckett, Samuel. *The unnameable.* (English edition) New York: Grove Press, 1958

Buber, Martin. *Tales of the Hasidim.* Vol. 1 New York: Schocken, 1991.

Buechner, Frederick. *Wishful Thinking: A Theological ABC.* San Francisco: Harper & Row, 1993.

Carlson, Eric. *Born That Way.* Eversham: Arthur James, 1952.

Carney, Dana, Amy J. C. Cuddy, and Andy J. Yap. "Power Posing: Brief Non-Verbal Displays Affect Neuroendocrine Levels and Risk Tolerance." *Psychological Science XX(X) 1–6* (Journal of the Association for Psychological Science) September 21, 2010. DOI: 101177/0956797610383437

Castle, Tony. *The Hodder Book of Christian Quotations.* London: Hodder and Stoughton, 1982

Coombes, Heather. "Tenaciously Yours." *Australian Rehabilitation Review* 5, no. 1 (1981) 25–30

Covey, Stephen R. *The 8th Habit: From Effectiveness to Greatness.* New York: Free Press, 2005.

Croucher, Rowland, ed. *Still Waters, Deep Waters: Meditations and Prayers for Busy People.* Sydney: Albatross Books, 1987.

Foer, Jonathan Safran. "How Not to Be Alone." *New York Times Sunday Review,* June 8, 2013 *http://www.nytimes.com/2013/06/09/opinion/ sunday/how-not-to-be-alone.html?_r=0*

Hardy, Graham W. *Another Minute Please*. Sydney: A. H. & A. W. Reed, 1979.

Johnson, Jan. *Abundant Simplicity: Discovering the Unhurried Rhythms of Grace*. Downers Grove, IL: IVP Books, 2011.

Lesslie, Robert D. *Angels on the Night Shift*. Eugene, OR: Harvest House, 2012.

———. *Notes from a Doctor's Pocket*. Eugene, OR: Harvest House, 2013.

McCallum, Tim. "Dreaming the Impossible Dream" *Focus on Independence* (Newsletter of Independence Australia, Collingwood, Vic. Spring Edition 2015) Mundy, Linus. *Slow-Down Therapy*. St Meinrad, IN: Abbey Press, 1990.

Newbigin, J. E. Lesslie. "Not Whole Without the Handicapped." In *Partners in Life: The Handicapped and the Church*, edited by Geiko Muller-Fahrenholz, 17–25. Geneva: WCC Publications, 1979.

Nouwen, Henri J. M. *The Road to Daybreak*. New York: Doubleday, 1990.

———. *The Wounded Healer: Ministry in Contemporary Society*. New York: Doubleday, 1972.

Phillips, Vera and Edwin H. Robertson. *J. B. Phillips: The Wounded Healer*. Grand Rapids, MI: Eerdmans, 1985.

Rozakis, Laurie. "Chapter 23: Speaking Off-the-Cuff" *The Complete Idiot's Guide to Public Speaking* 2nd edition New York: Alpha, 1999.

Spink, Kathryn. *The Wisdom of Mother Teresa*. Oxford: Lion Publishing, 1998.

Watkinson, Walter L. "The Invincible Strategy," in *The Supreme Conquest and other Sermons Preached in America* New York: F.H. Revell, 1907.

Wolterstorff, Nicholas. *Lament for a Son*. Grand Rapids, MI: William Eerdmans, 1987.

Endnotes

Chapter 1

1   Quoted in *Quotesgram*
     http://quotesgram.com/img/warren-buffett-quotes/6530268/
     Accessed October 11, 2016.

Chapter 5

1   Frederick Buechner, *Wishful Thinking: A Theological ABC* (San
     Francisco: Harper & Row, 1993).
2   William Barclay, *The Gospel of Matthew: Volume 1: Chapters
     1–10*. Revised edition (Edinburgh: St Andrew Press, 1975) 177.
3   Samuel Beckett, *The Unnameable*. English ed. (New York:
     Grove Press, 1958)

Chapter 7

1   Kathryn Spink, *The wisdom of Mother Teresa*. (Oxford: Lion
     Publishing, 1998) 29.

Chapter 10

1   Order of Saint Benedict, The rule of Benedict: (English) an
     index to texts online and gateway to RB bibliographic index
     Chapter 53.

http://www.osb.org/rb/text/rbemjo3.html#53 Accessed October 10, 2016.

2   Order of Saint Benedict, The rule of Benedict: (English) an index to texts online and gateway to RB bibliographic index Chapter 48.

http://www.osb.org/rb/text/rbemjo3.html#48 Accessed October 10, 2016.

3   The source of this quotation is unknown.

Chapter 12

1   Stephen R. Covey, *The 8th Habit: From Effectiveness to Greatness* (New York: Free Press, 2005), 191.

2   The source of this quotation is unknown.

Chapter 14

1   The source of this quotation is unknown.

2   As quoted in Richard Rohr, "The Sacred Wound," *Richard Rohr's Daily Meditation,* Center for Action and Contemplation, posted October 16, 2015

https://cac.org/the-sacred-wound-2015-10-16/ Accessed October 8, 2016.

3   Richard Rohr "The Power of Powerlessness", *Richard Rohr's Daily Meditation,* Center for Action and Contemplation, posted November 16, 2015

https://cac.org/the-power-of-powerlessness-2015-11-16/ Accessed October 8, 2016.

4   As quoted in *Brainy Quote*

http://www.brainyquote.com/quotes/ authors/m/meister_eckhart. html Accessed October 11, 2016.

5   As quoted in Tony Castle *The Hodder Book of Christian Quotations* (London: Hodder and Stoughton, 1982) Quote: H253, 121.

6   As quoted in *Goodreads*

http://www.goodreads.com/quotes/1273084-don-t-shine-so-others-can-see-you-shine-so-that Accessed October 11, 2016.

7   As quoted in *Goodreads http://www.goodreads.com/quotes/41181-i-am-a-hole-in-a-flute-that-the-christ-s* Accessed October 11, 2016.
8   The source of this quotation is unknown.
9   As quoted in *Brainy Quote http://www.brainyquote.com/quotes/quotes/b/bessieande140896.html* Accessed October 11, 2016.
10   Dietrich Bonhoeffer, "Who am I?" *DBonhoeffer.org http://www.dbonhoeffer.org/who-was-db2.htm* Accessed October 8, 2016.

Appendix A

1   J. E. Lesslie Newbigin, "Not Whole Without the Handicapped," in *Partners in Life: The Handicapped and the Church* ed. Geiko Muller-Fahrenholz (Geneva: WCC Publications, 1979), 25.

Appendix D

1   Carlson, Eric. *Born That Way.* (Eversham: Arthur James, 1952).
2   Laurie Rozakis, "Chapter 23: Speaking Off-the-Cuff" *The Complete Idiot's Guide to Public Speaking* 2nd edition (New York: Alpha, 1999) 228.

Appendix E

1   Dana Carney, Amy J. C. Cuddy and Andy J. Yap, "Power Posing: Brief Non-Verbal Displays Affect Neuroendocrine Levels and Risk Tolerance" in *Psychological Science* (Journal of the Association for Psychological Science) September 21, 2010. DOI: 101177/0956797610383437.
2   26 Martin Buber, *Tales of the Hasidim* Vol. 1 (New York: Schocken, 1991), 25.
3   27 Tim McCallum, "Dreaming the Impossible Dream" *Focus on Independence* (Newsletter of Independence Australia, Collingwood, Vic. Spring Edition 2015).
4   As quoted in *Wikiquote, https://simple.wikiquote.org/wiki/Creighton_Abrams* Accessed October 14, 2016.

5   Linus Mundy, *Slow-Down Therapy* (St Meinrad, IN: Abbey Press, 1990) 25.

6   As quoted in Robert D. Lesslie, *Notes from a Doctor's Pocket* (Eugene, OR: Harvest House, 2013), 20.

7   W. L. Watkinson's sermon "The Invincible Strategy," in *The Supreme Conquest and other Sermons Preached in America* (New York: F.H. Revell, 1907) 218.

8   Nicholas Wolterstorff, *Lament for a Son* (Grand Rapids, MI: Wm Eerdmans, 1987) 26.

9   As quoted in *Quote Investigator: exploring the origins of quotations http://quoteinvestigator.com/2010/06/29/be-kind /* Accessed October 13, 2016.

10   As quoted in Jonathan Foer, "How Not to Be Alone," *New York Times Sunday Review* June 8, 2013 *http://www.nytimes.com/2013/06/09/opinion/sunday/how-not-to-be-alone.html?_r=0 /* Accessed October 8, 2016.

11   ibid.

Appendix F

1   Sarah McKay, "These Are the 7 Habits of Highly Healthy Brains (In Order of Importance)," *Everyday Neuroscience for Brain Health and Wellness* (blog), January 22, 2016. *http://yourbrainhealth.com.au/ these-are-the-7-habits-of-highly-healthy-brains-in-order-of-importance/*

2   Term inspired by Robert D. Lesslie, *Angels on the Night Shift* (Eugene, OR: Harvest House, 2012).

Appendix G

1   Virtues for Life: The Heart of Everyday Living "Two wolves" *http://www.virtuesforlife.com/two-wolves/*Accessed October 13, 2016.

2   As quoted in "Mountain Wings Devotional Issue No. 15191, Genius" *Mountain Wings.* *http://www.mountainwings.com/pics/0049_genius-mw.jpg /* Accessed October 13, 2016.

Appendix H

1   As quoted in "Mountain Wings Devotional Issue No. 3317, Tooth and Nail" *Mountain Wings* / *http://www.mountainwings. com/past/3317.htm* Accessed October 13, 2016.

2   As quoted in Rowland Croucher, ed., *Still Waters: Deep Waters: Meditations and Prayers for Busy People* (Sydney: Albatross Books, 1987), 28.

3   As quoted in Jan Johnson, *Abundant Simplicity: Discovering the Unhurried Rhythms of Grace* (Downers Grove, IL: IVP Books, 2011), 55.

4   Reinhold Neibuhr, "Serenity Prayer," *Beliefnet http://www. beliefnet. com/prayers/protestant/addiction/serenity-prayer.aspx* / Accessed October 13, 2016.

5   Tony Alessandra, "Dr T's timely tips: No. 28: Abraham Lincoln: Leadership Genius: A Leader Always Fails Upwards" *Alessandra. com* (official site) *http://www.alessandra.com/timelytips1/28.asp* Accessed October 13, 2016.

6   Kathryn Spink, op. cit. 33.

7   Ibid.

8   Richard Rohr, "Modern Peacemakers" *Richard Rohr's Daily Meditation*, October 31, 2015.
https://cac.org/modern-peace-makers-weekly-summary-2015-10-31/

9   Op cit. Spink, 37.

10   Dietrich Bonhoeffer, "Who am I?" *DBonhoeffer.org http://www. dbonhoeffer.org/who-was-db2.htm* Accessed October 8, 2016.

11   Graham Hardy, *Another Minute Please* (Sydney: A. H. & A. W. Reed, 1979), 48.